CURVY BRIDES OF BLOSSOM FORD

BOOKS 5-8

IRIS WEST

Curvy Brides Of Blossom Ford Books 5-8

Copyright 2023 Iris West

All rights reserved.

This is a work of fiction. Any references to historical events, real people, or real places are used fictitiously. Other names, characters, places and events are products of the author's imagination, and any resemblance to actual events or persons living or dead is entirely coincidental.

No part of this book may be reproduced in any form or by any electronic or mechanical means, including information storage and retrieval systems, without permission in writing from the author. The only exception is by a reviewer, who can quote a short excerpt in a review.

FREE BOOK

Would you like a free book? Sign up to my mailing list at https://dl.bookfunnel.com/t191w45ryj to receive a copy of Loving My Fake Husband, a Curvy Brides of Blossom Ford Series short story and updates on upcoming books, giveaways and more.

MARRYING THE WIDOWED DOCTOR

CURVY BRIDES OF BLOSSOM FORD BOOK 5

IRIS WEST

Chapter 1

Liam

I USED TO THINK middle age crisis was an excuse to do crazy things. However, I'm starting to believe it is a thing. Nothing else, rational that is, can explain the fact that I'm considering marrying a woman matched to me by a matchmaking agency, only a few days after my forty-first birthday. Especially when the woman I loved and built a family with has only been gone three and a half years.

My hands tighten around a picture of Lucy smiling, taken before our marriage, her auburn hair flying, and once again the certainty that I have to follow through with this marriage, however crazy it is, solidifies in me. I have to keep the promise she forced me to make on our wedding night; I would find someone to love and be a mom for our children if anything happened to her.

Loving is out of the question. Never again do I want to go through the agonizing pain of losing a woman I love. Besides, even if it's possible to fall in love again, how can I live with the kind of happiness I shared with Lucy when she's not here?

I can, however, fulfill the mom part.

"Daddy, Ollie is pulling my hair." Olivia hides behind me as her twin brother chases her.

I place the picture on a shelf and pick up my four-year-olds, one on each arm. They give me the strength to keep the silly promise I made. I first started thinking about marriage when the twins were three and turned into monsters. Their nanny fell pregnant and quit to be a full-time mom.

None of the nannies that came afterwards could control them or deal with the uncertainty of the long hours I worked, when urgent surgeries became necessary. Then a couple of weeks ago, during Christmas dinner at Lucy's parents in New York, Olivia declared Santa was bad because he hadn't provided the first present on her list–a mom.

I want to do everything I can to make Liv and Ollie happy. That's what I'll focus on. It's the only way to make sense of me going ahead with an arranged marriage.

The bell rings.

"Be nice to the lady and each other." I place the kids on the floor beside a pile of toys. Squaring my shoulders, I march to the door and open it.

The smile of welcome freezes on my face. My breath hitches. Large sea-green eyes set in an oval-shaped face with the most kissable lips I've ever seen stare up at me for what seems like ages before I realize I'm staring back. The picture the agency sent didn't do justice to the curvy woman standing in the cold. The honey of her cheeks and the black of her long coat give the snow-covered garden color.

"Miss. Clark?"

She nods.

I move aside to let her pass, then take her coat. In tight-fitting black jeans and a red blouse that complements smooth honeyed skin, her curves are even more alluring. So is the scent of roses coming from her. My cock stirs.

Calm down and breathe.

I hung up the coat, and stride to the sitting room, annoyed at my reaction. It's unwanted and improper. In the last three and a half years, I've come across many attractive women, yet I never showed the slightest interest. Why now when I'm about to check whether Angel Clark would make an excellent mother for my kids?

The moment she spots the twins, she heads straight for them, sits cross-legged on the floor near them and says hi.

They watch her. A couple of minutes pass. Ollie traipses to her. Grabs her ponytail with his chubby hands and pulls. Angel reaches for him, tickles until he's giggling and releases her hair. He falls onto her lap, squirming.

"That's the consequence of pulling my hair. I won't stop tickling." There is laughter in Angel's face and her hands are gentle.

My lips tug up when Liv moves closer to the duo on the floor, hazel eyes identical to her brother's, wide open.

"Are you big sister Liv?" Angel asks.

Olivia nods.

"I'm Miss. Angel." She stretches out a hand.

Liv's eyes move from the hand to Ollie, who's still sitting on Angel's lap, then back to the hand. She shakes it.

Warmth spreads through my chest. Ollie and Liv fight like cats and dogs, but Liv is very protective of her brother. Although they are only a few minutes apart, he's developing at a much slower pace than her. Pleasing him is one way to get on her good side.

"He's Ollie." Liv sits in front of Angel, copies her cross-legged pose and studies her.

"I have to talk to Miss Angel, so come and draw," I say to the twins after they've had a little chat with Angel.

I settle Liv and Ollie in the kitchen with crayons and drawing pads. When I return to the sitting room, Angel is gazing at the photos spread all over the room of me and Lucy with the kids at different ages. In the most recent picture, the twins are six months old.

I sit and switch the monitor to listen to the kids, but my eyes stray to Angel as soon as I'm done.

"I love Liv and Ollie," she says once she joins me in the sitting area.

That is something I like about her. How direct and decisive she is, despite being only twenty-four. I noticed it in her short profile statement and that, together with the fact she stated she's more interested in being a full-time mom rather than having a husband, is the reason I chose her. Her experience as a childcare provider is a bonus I'm grateful for.

"They like you. They rarely take to strangers. What do you think about the marriage now?"

A blush tints her cheeks, making me wonder what she's thinking. She turns away and studies a picture of the kids.

"I'll go ahead." She gazes at me, but I can't make the expression in her eyes.

"We have a deal, then."

Most of the paperwork for preparing the marriage, including a contract, was done online. She wanted to meet Liv and Ollie, and I had to see how the three of them interacted before making a final decision and signing the contract.

As the kids and I see Angel out, I remind myself why I'm marrying her–to get a mom for my kids. The reason I couldn't stop my eyes from watching the way her ass fit those tight jeans as she put her coat on was the three and a half years of celibacy my body endured. I may not be able to control the way I react to Angel, but that's okay, because my heart suffered so much after losing Lucy, it knows not to fall in love again.

Chapter 2

Angel

I'VE DREAMED OF THIS day since I was a little girl; marrying a handsome groom I love and can rely on with my family and friends around me. Liam Johnson is the sexiest man I've ever seen and I'm already half in love with him and the way he cares for Liv and Ollie. The brilliant neurosurgeon will have no trouble providing for our family, too. But he doesn't love me.

Dad pats my hand. His sea-green eyes are steady as he looks at me. The butterflies in my tummy settle a little. As the wedding march song starts, I gaze at my flower girl and ring boy, Liv and Ollie, walking ahead of me. More butterflies settle. They are the reason I signed up for a marriage of convenience.

An accident when I was young left me unable to have kids. After my long-term boyfriend broke up with me because he realized he wanted to have his own kids rather than adopting, a marriage of convenience became the only viable option I could think of.

IRIS WEST

When my eyes fix on Liam, I almost stop. He looks gorgeous in a tailored suit the color of his dark blue eyes. His shoulders are square, and he has that steady presence Dad always exudes. My nerves finally calm, but awareness of him as a man has my core clenching. Heat creeps up my neck towards my cheeks as I remember the hot dreams I've been having since I met him at his house just over a week ago. Taking in a long breath, I command myself to focus on the kids I already think of as mine and the friends and family in the registry office.

As soon as I reach the altar, all I can think about is Liam again. The moment his steady gaze fixes on me, I'm trapped. I try to concentrate on the words Mrs. Green, the officiant, is saying, as this is a special moment. I've been to a few friends and family weddings and always thought of the day my time would come.

"I take this woman to be my lawfully wedded wife from this day forward," Liam says in his deep voice when Mrs. Green prompts him.

My heart races. I don't think I'll ever forget these words or the way his voice sounded when he stated them, strong like he was promising himself I was his to care for, like he's pledging the words to his inner self.

A shiver runs through me. Mrs. Green clears her throat. I realize it's my time to say the vows. In the strongest voice I can manage, I say the words back to Liam.

His best man and colleague Jamal, also a widower, helps Ollie bring the ring to us. My eyes tear when the little boy stretches his hands out, his ivory, chubby cheeks puffed out with importance.

Liam takes my hand and slides the ring down my finger. His hands are firm; I can't help remembering what they were doing in my dream the night before. I'm not as steady as him when it's my turn to put the ring on him.

"You may kiss the bride," Mrs. Green's voice is filled with joy and anticipation.

Liam's eyes are a stormy blue as he gazes at me and slowly leans forward. I stand on my tiptoes. When his lips finally touch mine, they are soft and warm. Heat ignites in my pussy and I want a deeper touch. Liam pulls back. He watches me like he wants more. Then he blinks and that passionate stare is gone.

Mrs. Green congratulates us, and a teary Granny comes up and envelops me in her arms.

"Penny, you'll ruin her dress," Mrs. Green says.

"Now the wedding is done, the dress needs ruining." Granny wiggles her brows, making everyone laugh.

I'm sure I'm as red as a tomato now. I pick up Ollie and ruffle his hair. Then my work mates surround me, and a little sadness fills me. I've worked at Smart Teddies Day Care Center for six years. Since my high school friends left Blossom Ford to attend college and settled out of town, my work mates have become close friends. I'm going to miss them and the kids at daycare.

"Be happy Angel. Thank you for everything you've done for me and my little boy," Willow whispers when the others are congratulating Liam.

I hug her, glad that my new friend is looking so well. She was a bruised rag doll when she first came to Blossom Ford a year ago.

Mom calls out to everyone to pose for a picture and, of course, she wants photos outside, even though it's freezing, and everyone is complaining of the late January cold.

I'm sure Liam would've preferred foregoing all ceremonies, but he's smiling with Granny and Dad. Even when we have our first dance to a slow song in the marquee set up in our large backyard, he's a gentleman.

"You're a wonderful dancer," I say after he twirls me and catches my waist, neatly preventing a fall.

I watch his face light up, the crinkles around his eyes giving them a youthful look.

This is what he must have always looked like before his wife passed.

"You follow easily."

He twirls me again, and a thrill runs through me. By the time the music stops, I'm not sure if I'm glad or sad. Isn't it dangerous for me to love his company too much?

But when he wipes a crumb of cake off the side of my mouth after feeding me a forkful, I know protecting my heart is going to be an uphill battle.

I feed him back to loud cheers. Then, I'm dragged onto the small dance floor by my friends for a lively song.

"Your family is lovely," Liam says when we have a moment to ourselves after he's danced with Mom, Granny and some of my friends.

"I guess it's hard for us to do quiet. You don't mind all the rituals, do you?"

"Liv and Ollie have been having fun." He looks to where the twins are playing with a small group of kids. "They're loving having another set of grandparents, too. I think they are going to be very spoiled. I haven't had this much fun in a long time."

It'd be easier to keep my heart intact if he weren't kind. I wanted a beautiful wedding like this, but my parents and Granny, who only have one child and grandchild, would have been heartbroken if they hadn't been able to have at least this small celebration when I married. If it had been up to them, everyone in town would have received an invitation and the reception would be at the best wedding venue in town.

The fact Liam is doing everything to make sure I have a memorable wedding that my family can be proud of, tugs at my heartstrings and I want him to be truly mine. However, he was clear from the beginning of our arrangement that he wasn't looking for love. A mother for his children, companionship, and a sexual partner were all he wanted. He'd made it clear his heart wasn't available.

Chapter 3

Liam

IT'S PAST MIDNIGHT. I should be exhausted, yet all I can think about is the woman lying in bed with me, smelling of roses. It's a fragrance I'm growing very fond of and have begun to associate with Angel.

The kids were asleep when we arrived home. They didn't even wake up as we carried them into their bedroom and tucked them in bed.

Angel and I took turns using the bathroom. I thought she'd be tired, and suggested we sleep, even though the amount of skin her red camisole and shorts exposed made my dick stand to attention.

Her scent and knowing her honeyed skin and kissable lips are only an arm's length away, drove me straight to a raging hard-on. I've been breathing regularly for the past half-hour, trying to control myself, but every time I think I'm getting a handle on my body, she moves.

"Are you asleep?" Her voice is soft.

I turn to her. My eyes adjusted to the moonlight in the room long ago. I lie on my side, facing her.

"No. Are you tired?" I can't control the need in my voice.

She shakes her head.

"I can't stop thinking about touching you," I say.

I can't make out her expression. There isn't enough light.

"Me too." She lies on her side as well. "We are married."

A laugh escapes me. I really like how pragmatic she is. I switch on the bedside lamp. Her lips are tugged up. With the tip of one finger, I trace them. She bites the finger and my cock jerks.

I close the distance between us and kiss her. Her arms snake around my neck as she angles her head.

"I've wanted to do this since the moment I saw you," I whisper against her mouth when I come up for air.

"Don't stop then."

Laughter ripples through me until her nails scrape across my back. I remove my t-shirt. I want those nails on my skin.

She slips her camisole off too, freeing two large, rounded breasts with dusky, almost black nipples. They are so pretty; a little pre-cum spills off me.

I kiss each tip reverently. Then take one into my mouth and suck, pulling strongly.

"Yes, Liam."

"You like?" I rub my lips against the hard tip, take her other nipple into my mouth, licking it like candy before I suck on it.

A moan and another rake down my back are the answer.

I stroke up the sides of her chest, then slip my hand past the swell of her tummy. I grab her shorts and panties and pull them down her beautiful, thick legs, then quickly strip my sweatpants.

I want this night to be good for Angel. She's given up on having a husband who's in love with her, but there's no reason she can't have great sex.

"You're beautiful!" I'm not just saying it to please her. I'm so turned on by her curves, taking time to please her won't be easy.

"You too." She's looking at my cock like it's her favorite dessert.

I play with the soft curls on her mound, then pet her clit until she's undulating against my finger. Her nub is so hard, I want to taste it. I lick it twice, then take it into my mouth and suck hard. I slip two fingers into her wet pussy, then a third, and pump in and out of her.

"That's so good," she hums.

Her hands are tight around my neck, pulling me to her. Right now, there's no place I'd rather be. With a cry, Angel comes apart, convulsing against my mouth and hand. I slide up her body and kiss her, loving the way she looks right now, her sea-green eyes cloudy with pleasure and her face relaxed with satisfaction.

I place my aching cock against her folds and bury myself to the hilt in her, her juices and my pre-cum easing my penetration. Even so, she's so tight around me; I groan. The sensation of her firm hands stroking my ass drives more pleasure through me. I set a fast pace, a wave of relief filling me as Angel meets my every thrust.

She wraps her legs around me, allowing me to bury deeper into her with each thrust.

"Liam," Angel shouts against my neck.

I slip a hand between us and stroke her clit.

She contracts around my cock, her legs tightening around my ass, and I come violently, bucking as a stream of hot cum jets into her pussy. When I'm spent, it takes all my energy to roll over, so she's lying on top of me, and my dead weight is not pressing on her.

"Okay?"

Her upper body shakes against my chest. It takes me a few seconds to realize she's chuckling.

"I'm much more than okay. I think I got myself a very skillful husband in the bedroom department."

My laugh comes from deep inside me. It's loud, unrestrained and surprises me a little. It's been a long time since I laughed like this.

"And I got myself a beautiful, sexy wife who drives me to distraction and is so responsive to my touch, I'm afraid I'll be spending way too much time thinking about bed-time."

As I fall asleep, a wash of gratitude for Angel comes over me. With her, I can have great sex and maybe friendship while Liv and Ollie get a terrific mom. Angel seems to already love them and enjoyed having sex with me. Our hearts are not at all involved. Already, our contract marriage is getting off to an excellent start.

Chapter 4
Angel

I WAKE UP to muscular arms wrapped around me. Rays of sunshine slip through the curtains, illuminating the room. What we did last night flashes through my mind and a wave of pleasure ripples through me.

Large hands glide through my back and cup my butt cheeks, fondling them. I shiver again. It would be brilliant if I could wake up like this every day. I snake my hand past Liam's hard abdomen and circle his semi-hard cock.

"Good morning," I whisper. I turn my head so I'm looking at him. His eyes are closed. I slide my hand up and down his length.

"It's a delightful morning," his voice is strained.

Sounds come from the monitor.

"Let's go wake Daddy and Mommy."

Rustling noises follow.

I release Liam. He pulls away from me. Red suffuses his cheeks. He looks cute and unlike his usual assured self; I chuckle.

"It's not funny. They'll be here any minute."

"If they ask, we can say we undressed because we were hot."

Liam helps me look for my clothes and finds my camisole and panties. We put our underwear on before Liv's voice sounds outside the door. Like naughty children, we jump under the covers. The door bursts open.

"Daddy, are you awake?" Liv calls out loudly.

Both children run to the bed and climb on.

"Didn't you sleep? You woke up too early," Liam says to the kids after we've greeted them.

They tuck themselves in between us, their eyes wide with interest.

"Silly Daddy. The sun is shining. It's morning," Liv says.

"I'm hungry," Ollie cries, rubbing his tummy.

Liam looks at me, black curls tousled, eyes full of resignation. As much as I want the pleasure I know he can dish out, I'm fascinated by the picture the four of us make.

"How about pancakes and eggs?" I ask the three of them.

The kids cheer and scramble over Liam in their rush to get out of bed.

"I'm going to use the toilet first. I'll be there in a minute," I say.

Liam strolls out with them, holding a child in each arm. They say nothing about his navy boxers, but I stare at his butt until he catches me looking when he turns to close the door. I hide my face under the blankets, a little embarrassed by how much I want him.

When I'm alone, I get out of bed, wash quickly, and slip on my favorite old jeans and a snug sweater. In the kitchen, Liv and Ollie are sitting at the table with small glasses of orange juice in front of them. Liam is rummaging through cupboards.

"I have all the ingredients here," he says.

When I'm within touching distance of him, he leans closer. "I'm going to wash and get dressed."

"What are you hiding, Daddy?" Ollie asks.

"Mommy and Daddy stuff," Liv's whisper is so loud I can hear it.

A silly grin spreads over my face, but I don't care. For a while, when I found out I couldn't have children, I didn't think I'd ever hear anyone call me mom. That devastated me. I was only sixteen, but even though some of my friends couldn't understand my decision, I knew I wanted to be just like my mom and be a full-time mother and homemaker.

Liam ruffles the twins' hair as he leaves the kitchen, and my heart explodes with happiness. I'm in love with him. He's generous to me and respectful of my family. I love how he's so affectionate to his kids and adores them, and I love his gorgeous body.

Liam strolls out with them, holding a child in each arm. They say nothing about his navy boxers, but I stare at his butt until he catches me looking when he turns to close the door. I hide my face under the blankets, a little embarrassed by how much I want him.

When I'm alone, I get out of bed, wash quickly, and slip on my favorite old jeans and a snug sweater. In the kitchen, Liv and Ollie are sitting at the table with small glasses of orange juice in front of them. Liam is rummaging through cupboards.

"I have all the ingredients here," he says.

When I'm within touching distance of him, he leans closer. "I'm going to wash and get dressed."

"What are you hiding, Daddy?" Ollie asks.

"Mommy and Daddy stuff," Liv's whisper is so loud I can hear it.

A silly grin spreads over my face, but I don't care. For a while, when I found out I couldn't have children, I didn't think I'd ever hear anyone call me mom. That devastated me. I was only sixteen, but even though some of my friends couldn't understand my decision, I knew I wanted to be just like my mom and be a full-time mother and homemaker.

Liam ruffles the twins' hair as he leaves the kitchen, and my heart explodes with happiness. I'm in love with him. He's generous to me and respectful of my family. I love how he's so affectionate to his kids and adores them, and I love his gorgeous body.

He's such a straight-forward person, that even though he can't give me his heart, as long as we can have a friendly relationship and love the kids together, I'll be happy. I'll just have to make sure he doesn't find out about my feelings. I don't want our relationship to be awkward when he was clear from the beginning love wasn't a part of our marriage.

Friends with benefits, that's what we'll be. I can do it.

I realize the kids are gazing at me.

"Who wants to make pancakes?"

I move the ingredients to the table so they can help and search through drawers until I find overalls, then help Liv and Ollie put them on.

Liam saunters back into the kitchen, also wearing a sweater and jeans, his hair wet and slicked back.

"I'm not sure about this." His eyes widen when Ollie grabs the bag of flour.

"If you join in, it'll be fun."

He rushes to his boy's side and helps him scoop out the flour.

"How much?" He asks Ollie, who looks at me.

"About half."

I'm helping Liv crack the eggs into a small bowl when a chortle and a muffled curse breaks my concentration. Ollie is giggling; his hands are white, and bits of flour are stuck to his head. He's pointing to his dad, who also has flour on parts of his body.

Liv joins in. I try not to, but Liam looks so struck I can't help it. I crack up. He takes a while to see the funny side of this spectacle, but soon, he's chuckling too.

Chapter 5

Liam

"CAN YOU CLOSE HER up?" I ask my assistant neurosurgeon.

"Of course," Lori answers, a glint in her eye I know too well. We've been operating for twelve hours, yet she wouldn't dream of saying no, even if she had a choice. She's one of the best fellows that's ever worked under me and reminds me of myself in the way she's married to her patients and spends so much time at the hospital. With crazy surgeries like these, it's no wonder the twins' nannies couldn't handle the unpredictability of my hours and quit often.

Before we had the twins, Lucy was so engrossed in her art sometimes I'd get home after being away most of the day and she'd be surprised when I arrived, completely unaware of the passage of time. It was frustrating, but the way she could focus on a particular task for so long was one of the things that fascinated me about her. After the babies were born, our nanny was always around, still I sometimes wonder if Lucy wanted me home more often.

"The operation was successful. We excised the tumor. Have a well-deserved rest, so you can care for your wife when she's awake," I say to my patient's husband.

I stretch my arms and circle my shoulders and neck as I head to my office. There's an excellent coffee machine there, a present Lucy gifted me when we moved to Blossom Ford five years ago, however I'm too tired to wait and grab an expresso from a vending machine. I quickly take care of paperwork and leave the hospital by nine.

Outside Weston-Parker General, I head east towards home to a part of town under the mountains of Blossom Ford. Lucy fell in love with the area and although the house she wanted required lengthy renovations, she insisted we buy it. We lived on the other side of town, near Blossom Ford Point for the year it took to renovate and decorate the house the way she wanted to.

It's still hard how she passed six months after Liv and Ollie were born, from a car accident, only days before our move in date. I blink and blink again. Every day, things like a scent or painting remind me of her, but today, it was the worry on the face of my patient's husband, his fear that he'd lose her.

It takes fifteen minutes to get home from the hospital and soon I'm pulling into the driveway. Anticipation runs through me when I think of Angel waiting for me inside and having a meal with her. She's on her knees in the sitting room, peering behind the sofa. My eyes lock on the way her ass fills out the soft pants she's wearing and just like that, I want her. That's all it takes, a look, touch, or the sound of her voice.

"Got you!" She waves a soft toy in the air, spots me mid-celebration and smiles.

I march over, and pull her against me, the scent of roses and the feel of her soft body against mine so familiar, I'm thinking of moments like this at the end of a long day as home, even though we've only been married three weeks.

"Tough day?"

"Complex operation. The patient's tumor was large and in a difficult position. A tiny slip could have meant paralysis. The chances of survival weren't high either."

"I guess they were lucky they got the best neurosurgeon in the world."

Laughter bubbles out of me.

"That's what everyone says. I'm not being biased."

"Your Gran?"

"She knows everything that happens in Blossom Ford. Apparently, some nurses and female doctors are disappointed they missed out on marrying you. Now, get in the shower while I warm dinner. If we stay like this any longer, you might miss it again and Granny will start saying I'm not feeding you."

I laugh again as Angel extricates herself from our embrace and rushes to the kitchen, as if she's tempted to stay.

The twins are sleeping soundly when I open the door to the nursery, Liv on her tummy in her favorite pajamas and Ollie cuddling his toy. I shower quickly, eager to try out whatever Angel made today.

"This is amazing," I say after a bite of chili con carne and tuck into the rest of the food. "You can open a restaurant with skills like these." She told me she'd learned to cook from her gran and Mom.

"I love cooking! Caring for kids is my favorite thing to do though."

"How did you know you wanted to be a homemaker? And a childcare worker?"

She finishes her bite of food and sips wine. "Mom is the best in the world. I don't know if it's because she had me late in her life, but she cooked and baked with me, made sandcastles and dolls' clothing. Even though Dad was busy at work, on weekends we rode our bikes to Blossom Ford Point, watched movies, and hang out with Granny. I was loved so much, I wanted to give back to other children. I wanted to be like Mom."

There's a sparkle in Angel's eyes and an energy around her that makes me want to hear her talk.

"My parents divorced when I was six. I had a couple of stepfathers, but they were busy living their own lives. I assume Mom and Dad did things with me before things soured between them; I don't remember. Going fishing and to the ball game with your dad are the first father-son outings I remember. It's good to hear him call me son, too. And my colleagues love the scarves your mom makes for me."

"You know he's going to keep pestering you to support the local team, right? And just wait until Mom knits you jumpers."

The look of horror on her face is so comical; my lips lift.

"The ones she made Liv and Ollie are beautiful."

"They are cute on kids. Now imagine a bright yellow sweater with green and purple leaves on the front."

"I get it. Doesn't she make them for you? All your sweaters are beautiful."

Her face turns pink. I never thought I was the type that was attracted by a woman blushing, yet I get a kick out of seeing Angel's reaction whenever I compliment her.

"I have a couple of friends who love Mom's sweaters and live out of town. They steal them off me."

"You send it to them knowing they'll love them." I like the mix of sweetness and cheekiness in her personality.

"I've never heard you talk about your parents before."

"We're not very close. Mom is on her fourth husband. I believe Dad is on his fifth wife. I had nannies until I was about twelve. After I left for college, I only saw them twice. We exchange Christmas cards. That works for us."

Angel's eyes soften. She places one hand on mine, where it lies on the flowery tablecloth. "My parents will be yours, too. And if you ever want to get closer to yours, we can always visit them.

IRIS WEST

Maybe they want to spend more time with you, but it's been so long, they feel awkward about it."

My heart stutters.

I'm in love with this woman.

Chapter 6
Angel

A WEEK LATER, I'M having lunch with Willow at Jackson's Diner. Mom gets to spoil our kids rotten whilst I get a break from the twins and Willow enjoys her day off without a kid in tow.

"There's something about diner fries I love. I've been trying to cook healthy meals at home; it's nice to have this treat," I say, anticipation filling me as I stare at my loaded plate of cheeseburger and fries.

"I'd like to know what they put in this sauce. It'd sell fast, if it's bottled up."

I tuck into my food. "Old Jackson won't say. He's convinced someone will steal it from him. There's something different about you. Is it a man?"

Willow chokes on iced coke. I stretch across the small table and pat her back. Once the coughing fit passes, she shakes her head.

"Raising my little boy well is all that matters to me. He hasn't had a good start in life. I'm going to make sure he's happy."

For a moment she looks like she's about to say more, however her expression closes. That look is familiar. She won't say anything about her past, no matter how much I press.

"Blossom Ford's Matchmaking Agency has a one hundred percent success rate, if you ever want to try marriage, so Jaiden can have a dad. And you never know, you and your matched husband might fall in love. Granny says the Navajo blood of the women who run the agency has foreseeing abilities and that's why every couple they match always ends up falling in love." It seems I'm the only exception.

"Just like you? You're in love with your husband. I see it in the way you watch and talk about him. You get this look when you're thinking about him, too."

It's my turn to splutter.

"Am I that transparent? I thought it was only my family that saw it."

"Sorry," Willow says. "Something is wrong, though. You're not your usual self."

I wish I'd had more success when I tried to learn how to hide my feelings. Does Liam know I'm in love with him, too? I hope not. Yet, I can't get rid of the niggling suspicion that he's noticing my feelings for him. What else can explain the way he's become distant from me?

It started the night he came home late from work and opened up about his parents. For the first time since our wedding, we didn't make love. It's been a week since then and he still hasn't touched me. Every time I tried to get closer, he'd say he was tired. He's coming home later too and spends more time in his study, the only place in the house I'm not welcome. Where I suspect he spends time with the woman in his heart.

The twins have pictures of their mom in their bedroom, but the other rooms in the house have pictures of the four of us. I'm sure the study has pictures of the first Mrs. Johnson. That's why Liam told me he'd clean the room himself.

"It's nothing, really. I love being a mom and Liam is generous. He offered to get me help." I'm not ready to share what's happening with Liam.

"I bet that's not all he's generous with." She wiggles her thick brows.

"How does your mind go there? Honestly, Willow." I hide my face by taking a long sip of my drink.

"I don't think it's the sex. Whatever it is, I hope you guys sort it out. You're so right for each other. Maybe it's true that agency can really foresee the future of couples."

Liam and I are right for each other. If he only opened up his heart and gave us a chance, he might fall in love with me. The way we are so explosive in bed leaves no doubt he's attracted to me. He likes me too. I see it in the way he ensures I'm always comfortable and genuinely listens to me raving on about mom programs.

Of course, I knew his heart wouldn't be mine from the beginning. I'd accepted friendship and brilliant sex together with the joy of seeing the kids grow as a family was as much as I was going to get from him.

But now even our friendship is at risk, and I don't know what I did to cause him to distance himself from me.

Sure, I miss the heat of his touch. However, I miss our chats and the way he holds me in his arms even more.

Liam

I FORCE MYSELF to eat the baked potato in the cafeteria, frustration at how much I've allowed Angel to become a part of my life filling me. I endured the food at work for years. It took Angel's food four weeks to spoil me to the point where I compare the taste of everything I eat with her cooking.

She got into the habit of packing sandwiches for me, but Liv has had a fever for the past couple of days and Angel has been taking care of her nonstop. She usually wakes up when I leave for work yet didn't stir this morning.

Before I left for work, I watched her sleep, the longing to wrap her in my arms so strong, I had to drag myself to work.

"Poor potato," Jamal says as he pulls a chair opposite me and sits down, tucking into his own potato. He rotates his neck and shoulders.

I look at my plate. The potato is now an untidy pile of mash.

"Extensive surgery?" I ask, giving up on the food.

"Emergency patient. I came in at three in the morning. I have another surgery after lunch. There isn't much point going home. Besides, there's a new nurse in general surgery. She's pretty. Maybe she's the woman I'm meant to be with. I'm having coffee with her in a little while."

I stare at him. "You were in love with Roshelle. I didn't think you'd ever laugh again without her in your life. Falling in love a second time might cause you pain, again."

Jamal watches me, a somber look in his eyes. "I can only hope it doesn't. Even if it does, I'd rather be with someone for the months, years we have than live without love. It isn't easy to find that special person meant for you. It's even harder to find a second special person." He gulps half a bottle of water. "You found yours. If it happens to me, I'm not letting go, no matter how afraid I'll be to lose her again. If that's what's bothering you, I get it. I think I'd be the same. Just don't let that fear ruin your relationship. The way your eyes followed Angel on your wedding day, man, I hope I get to experience that again."

Was I that besotted even then?

I liked Angel from the beginning, but I didn't think it was possible for me to fall so deeply in love with another woman other than Lucy. Now I know what I feel for Angel is love. She's the first thing I think about when I wake up. I want to hear her talk about the mom programmes she loves so much. I'm dying with need for her.

"Won't you feel guilty?"

"About being happy without her?" Jamal asks so quietly, it's hard to hear him in the jumbled chatter of the busy cafeteria. "Don't know. Guess I will, when the sorrow of her going so young hits me. But that happens less and less. More and more, I remember the good times. She'd want me to be happy again. Lucy would want the same for you. If the situation were reversed, you'd never expect her to remain single."

We walk silently around the hospital until my afternoon clinic starts and it's time for Jamal to meet the new nurse.

In between patients, I can't stop wondering about what Jamal said. I've been thinking less and less about Lucy, even before meeting Angel. I suppose this made me feel a little guilty. Falling in love again intensified that guilt. Also, I've always vowed I wouldn't be like Mom and Dad. When I met Lucy, I didn't believe in marriage. We dated for years before I mustered up the courage to trust our marriage would last. I swore to myself I'd always be loyal to her.

It's true I'd want Lucy to find another love. Why am I not giving myself the same chance? And I was faithful to Lucy from the day we met to the day I married Angel.

Half-way through the afternoon, I check up on Angel. Relief floods me when I realize her tired voice is back to normal. The way her eyes cloud up when I avoid spending time with her has been killing me. I can't bear the desolation in those pretty eyes anymore. She deserves better. Somehow, I'll have to deal with the fear of being in pain if anything ever happens to her.

Chapter 7

Angel

I FROWN AS I spot Liam's car in the drive. It's only three o'clock. Officially, he finishes at six, even though lately he's been getting home close to ten or eleven.

Didn't he get my text that I'd be home?

While I was at Mom's, he called to say he'd forgotten a package was arriving today and wanted me home. We'd only just arrived, so Liv and Ollie refused to leave. Granny nearly pushed me out the door, uncharacteristically angry because she felt I wasn't trusting my family enough with my step kids. Which was utter rubbish.

Determined to have it out with her as soon as I receive the package and return to Mom's, I open the door. Maybe whatever Liam ordered is important and he can't wait to see it. If that is the case, I'll go back to Mom's while he waits for the delivery.

Although it's killing me, I'm trying to respect his wish to keep his heart for his first wife, but I don't know if I can survive losing our friendship. The tense atmosphere between us isn't good for the kids either. We've both looked cheerful around them, but if whatever's going on carries on for much longer, they'll notice. Kids are good at spotting these things. If I'm alone with Liam, I'm afraid I'll ask what's wrong before he's had time to deal with whatever made him change.

Before I turn into the kitchen, a flash of red catches my attention. There are rose petals on the floor. And I stepped on them without noticing. They lead to the sitting room. Soft music is coming from there as well.

"Liam?"

There's no answer. The scent of roses strengthens as I near the sitting room, just as I realize two of my favorite types of candles line the entrance. When I enter the room, my hand flies to my mouth.

One of Mom's large, multicolored picnic blankets is laid out in front of the fireplace. On it are plates of sandwiches, fruit, Granny's famous pumpkin pie, champagne and a few other treats.

A noise makes me turn. Liam is standing at the door, with an enormous balloon saying be my valentine and a bouquet of my favorite flowers in his other hand.

"Valentine's day was days ago," I blurt. How can I be thinking about how good he looks in the white button-down shirt he's wearing?

His eyes hold mine prisoner as he moves towards me, as if he's afraid I'll bolt. All I can do is stare at him.

"I've been a moron lately. That night, when I told you about my parents, I realized I'd fallen in love with you."

Already in a state at the thought of what this indoor picnic might mean, my heart goes into overdrive. I can't even speak.

"I don't." He stops, breathes in. "I don't want to hide anything from you. I was scared shitless of falling in love again and facing the possibility of loss. And I felt guilty towards Lucy. I'm sorry it's taken me a while to sort my feelings out and be the man you deserve."

A tear rolls down my cheek. "Liam," it's all I can say. My throat is crammed with cotton wool.

"I know love isn't part of our contract. If you want to keep it that way, I'll do everything I can to hide the way I feel about you and be happy with being friends and co-parents. Just let me hope one day your caring and attraction for me might turn into love."

I jump into his arms, not caring where the flowers and balloon fall when he catches me. I hold his dear face in my arms and kiss him, exhilarating at the familiar touch of his tongue against mine. It's as if I've come home.

"I love you," I say when I come up for air.

I smile at the wonder on his face.

"Since when?"

"When the agency sent me your photo, I figured I was going to have trouble not falling for you. The day after our wedding, I knew I was head over heels for you."

"God, I love you Angel." He nibbles on my lips. "I guess I should be romantic and make sure we have the picnic first."

He's now sucking on the pulse at my neck. He must have felt how fast it was beating.

"This is more romantic," I say before he devours my mouth.

He shuffles to the sofa without our mouths breaking contact, which is difficult when he's trying to avoid the picnic.

We strip before falling on the large sofa.

"I want you in my mouth. You've given me so much pleasure that way. I've only done it a few times."

"Woman, you're going to kill me. I'm aching for you."

He flips me so my pussy is hanging over his mouth and I'm facing his hard cock. I shiver when I see liquid seeping from the opening at the crown. I wasn't comfortable doing this with my ex boyfriend, but the few times I did it with Liam, he told me how to please him and was so vocal about enjoying my touch; my confidence has grown. My mouth waters. I'm surprised by how much taking him into my mouth turns me on.

He licks down the entire length of my slit. It feels amazing. My eyes close.

I envelop him in my mouth, stroking up, and down, my hands playing with his balls. He purrs, the vibration against my nub making me shiver again. When he takes my entire clit in his mouth and sucks softly while kneading my butt cheeks, I choke on his shaft and squeeze his balls hard.

Liam's cock falls out of my mouth as he flips me again. He places both my arms above me.

"I was enjoying that." I lick my lips.

His pupils are dilated and the blue in his eyes is as dark as I've ever seen them. He's close to the edge. It turns me on so much, tears sting my eyes. After the failure of my long-term relationship, I never thought I'd have something like this. No one can grow up in a family like mine without high self-esteem, but knowing Liam adores my voluptuous curves and can carry me so easily adds another level to my excitement.

"If you carry on, you're going to finish me in seconds," he bites out, holding my arms down.

"What's wrong with that?"

He lets go and kisses my eyes, lips and nose. The touch is so tender, my arms wrap around him. My chest is tight.

"I want to make love to you slowly, with our arms around each other, this first time, which seems like it's the first time for the rest of our times together."

He enters me languidly, breathing hard. I tangle my ankles with his legs, caressing them with my feet. His strokes are lazy and so is the glide of his tongue against mine.

I rake my hands up and down his back, enjoying the feel of his skin and the sense of being owned body and soul.

"My very own angel," Liam whispers against my neck, his lips pulling on the erogenous spot there.

"Yes, I'm yours," I cry against him.

By the time Liam increases the pace and rams into me, I'm a bundle of nerves. The moment he touches my clit, I come, his name a wordless cry.

"Angel!" His cry is loud as his cum shoots up my womb.

"The package," I whisper tiredly as Liam embraces me.

"There's no package. It was a ruse to get you here."

Granny's anger makes sense now. It was all pretense.

"Kids…"

"They are sleeping with your mom tonight."

My eyes shut in bliss.

Epilogue

Liam

Six years later

IT'S OUR SIXTH WEDDING anniversary, yet I never tire of gazing at Angel's soft honeyed face on my chest when I wake up. We got used to sleeping this way. Even on the occasional days I'm held up at the hospital and find her sleeping, we always end up this way when morning comes.

I'm not working today, and the twins are off school. They are trying to be quiet but are making such a racket; I wonder how Angel can sleep through it. She's still refusing to have help around the house and insists on driving the kids to their various clubs. Sometimes her mom, Granny and dad go with her. Although I walk our cocker spaniels Dolly and Rufus before work, they still take up a lot of her time. She insists on coming when I walk them after work. I suppose it's no wonder she's tired.

Three knocks sound on the door. It's Liv. She's so full of energy, she always goes overboard with everything she does.

Liv marches in, followed by the dogs, who are wagging their tails.

"Wow! Seriously?"

She turns away, and I laugh at the fake haughtiness on her shoulders.

"What is it?" Angel wakes and sits up just as the dogs bounce on the bed.

"Mom, I can't believe how you and Dad are still so lovey-dovey with each other. Ew!" She approaches the bed and lays a waterproof tablecloth on top of the cover. "Happy wedding anniversary," she sings to the accompaniments of the dogs' barking.

Ollie walks in wearing an overall, a large tray in his hands. He deposits it gently on the tablecloth and uncovers the plates.

"Happy anniversary, Mom and Dad," he says more quietly.

"This is lovely, sweethearts! It smells incredible too. Did you make the toast, Liv? It's browned just right," Angel says.

"See." Liv turns to Ollie. "Even Mom said so. It's perfect."

I stop myself from laughing at Ollie's raised eyebrow. I catch Angel's eye and know she's attempting the same thing. Our boy is so serious, that even though our doctor says he's growing well, I worry sometimes.

"What do you think, Dad?" Liv asks.

I gaze at Ollie. He shrugs. "It looks okay to me," I say, smiling at him.

Liv can't cook, no matter how much Angel teaches her. She has too much going in her brain to have the patience cooking requires. Her mind is full of information about stars, comics and the latest exploits into space.

Last year, when he was only nine, Ollie won the Blossom Ford Pumpkin Pie Contest. He was smart enough to do well at school if he applied himself, but his grades were average. He was happiest in Food Technology class. Not only had he memorized all the recipes his teacher and mom taught him; his cooking was to die for.

Liv and Ollie make themselves comfortable on the bed and we tuck into breakfast. It's become one of our traditions. Breakfast in bed on our wedding anniversary. This year was the first I didn't help the kids.

"Granny Jess sent a card," Olly states.

Angel was right about Mom. She'd wanted to spend more time together, but wasn't sure how. We'd never be as close as Angel's family. I feel closer to Angel's mom and dad, still we talk over the phone and see each other more. Dad is still gallivanting around the world, and I wish him well.

Every year, the kids spend a week of their summer break with Lucy's parents, so their biological mom is still a part of their lives. After we confessed our love for each other, Angel put a picture of the twins and Lucy in the sitting room, saying their mom would always be a part of our family.

"Happy anniversary, Hun," Angel says, her sea-green eyes sparkling.

"Happy anniversary, my angel."

I'm looking forward to spending the day alone with my very own angel when the kids go to their grandparents.

MARRYING THE SCARRED SOLDIER

CURVY BRIDES OF BLOSSOM FORD BOOK 6

IRIS WEST

Chapter 1
Willow

IF ANYONE HAD TOLD me I'd willingly put myself in a relationship again, I'd have laughed my head off. But here I am, in a secluded wooden cabin in the woods, married and willing at that. Out of the corner of my eyes, I take in my husband's massive shoulders, thick legs, almost shoulder length hair and beard. He's looking at the TV so I can't see his deep-set eyes and the other side of his face, yet, I've memorized their light gray color and the pink, rough looking skin on the right side of his face. A shiver runs through me.

Ransom turns toward me. I look away. Heat creeps up my face when I'm caught staring. I gaze at the cracking logs in the log burner and the heat in my body intensifies. I bite my lip. For years I didn't feel any desire and thought part of me had dried up with the bitterness from my past life, but the moment I laid eyes on Ransom a few months ago, lust stirred in me.

"Do you want to watch something else?"

His voice is deep, steady and quiet, just like him. It makes me think of strength and loyalty. As if it's the voice of someone I can trust. Which is bull considering his humongous size and bad boy look. Ransom Boyd is not the type of man a mother would look at and think of as a prospective husband for her daughter. That doesn't faze me because one, I don't have a mother or father, and two, I lived with the kind of white collar, handsome boy society believed made perfect husband material and went through hell.

"No, I like this." And I do like the soap that's playing. It's just that there's zero chance of me paying attention to it tonight. "I really don't mind if you want to watch something else, too." His profile from the matchmaking agency said he likes nature shows.

"Willow."

Even though I'm already looking at him, something in his voice and face makes me more alert.

"Didn't we decide we'd take turns choosing?" He asks.

I nod.

"It'll be my turn tomorrow. If I change the channel, you'll have two nights of watching animals in the wild. I won't let go of the remote."

His lip lifts a fraction. Is that an attempt at a joke? My own lips tug up.

"I'll keep the drama on." I lift the remote off the coffee table and put it on the armrest on my side of the couch. Then I pick it up and press pause. "Ask away if there's anything you want explained." I've watched a third of the show but I started it at the beginning so he won't feel lost.

Ransom scratches his beard. "Why did Michael say he committed the crime when he clearly didn't?"

I can't help the smile that tugs at my lips. "You'll see."

Suddenly, some of the tension in me disappears. He's watching. It may seem like a small thing, but to me, it's a step in the right direction for this marriage that's based on the small amount of information we exchanged about each other on the matchmaking agency profile and the couple of times we met. He's trying to get along with me.

The first time I saw Ransom was three months ago, which was about nine months after I arrived in Blossom Ford on the run from my partner of four years. I was shocked by the lust he stirred in me, but I didn't approach him. I was too busy surviving. Stopping myself thinking about him at night became a problem I couldn't solve, so I stopped trying and when I felt horny, it was his eyes and body I saw when I made myself come.

Six weeks ago, my high school friend Coleen called and said my ex-partner was looking for me again. For days, I was paralyzed with fear. My ex-partner had found me before when I run to Chicago. I'd thought being in a large city would make it almost impossible for him to find me, but I was wrong and barely escaped. I ran as far south as I could go until my money run out in Blossom Ford.

IRIS WEST

I made a home for me and my little boy, Jordan. He loves the friends he has made at Smart Teddies Day care, and I love my job there. I don't want to leave Blossom ford.

As I watched Jordan play on the swings at the park one Sunday, thinking about what to do, I sensed someone beside me. Terrified, I'd looked sideways. Granny Tallulah was sitting on the other side of the bench I was sitting on. I'd seen her wandering about town when I first arrived in Blossom Ford a few weeks later I learned she had dementia. Everyone in town looked out for her and walked her home if they found her out late at night or wandering the streets without shoes or a coat.

I think she thought I was her daughter because she always wanted to know what my little boy was eating and how he was doing and gave me advice to make him "big and strong" as she often said. That day, as I was leaving the park, Granny Tallulah grabbed my arm and said the strangest words. Her daughter would find me a husband who would protect me and my little boy. I remember the shiver that ran up my spine. Not even Angel, the closest friend I'd made in town, knew about my past.

As I headed home, I told myself Granny Tallulah was probably speaking generally, but the thought that the agency her daughter ran had matched a lot of happy couples in Blossom Ford, including a newlywed Angel and her husband, kept intruding into my mind. I signed up and when I was matched with Ransom; I recognized him straight away. The fact he was ex-military and lived in the mountains grabbed my attention and wouldn't let go. I started wondering if maybe he could protect us. That it'd be harder to be found in the mountains.

His profile said he was looking for companionship and love. I should have skipped past his picture because I wasn't looking for love. My ex-partner was my high school sweetheart. When I started living with him, I thought I'd at last found true happiness. Instead, I'd swapped the hell of bad foster care and a rough group home for the hell of an abusive partner.

I hadn't planned to mention anything when I met Ransom. The fear he'd change his mind about our arranged marriage after learning about my past was absolute. However, despite his rough looks, or maybe because of it, I'd sensed an honesty in Ransom that made me ashamed of lying to him. Suddenly, hiding my past didn't feel right, and I told him I was running from my ex.

"I spent almost all of my adult life protecting people. It's the one thing I'm good at," he'd said in that steady voice of his and although a part of me was terrified of trusting a man with my life, I didn't have many other choices and went ahead with the marriage.

Seeing him try to keep to the small arrangement we made about taking turns doing what we each like together gives me some hope of us getting along.

Chapter 2

Ransom

I'M NOT THE KIND of man to regret a decision I made, but a tiny part of me wonders if Willow would be better with a man who could give her the type of life she deserves. A beautiful woman like her shouldn't be with a scarred, reclusive man whose only company is books and animals. Problem is I've never been a gentleman. Now that Willow has decided to be my wife, I'm going to do everything in my power to make sure she never wants to leave.

Sitting on the sofa with her in my small living room feels good. Even though we're both nervous.

I've tried to make her as comfortable as possible, but I can tell she's not really watching the drama. And I don't blame her. What woman would feel comfortable on her first wedding night with a husband she's only met twice and doesn't know how to sweet talk her?

"Another beer?" As soon as the drama is over, I ask. I'm not trying to get her drunk; I just want her to relax a little.

Willow nods.

I pad to the kitchen area and grab us a couple of chilled bottles. My eyes run over every part of the small cabin. Checking everything is fine is a habit I can't get rid of, even though I retired from the military three years ago. Now that Willow and Jordan are here, there's a heightened sense of responsibility within me. Instead of feeling burdened by it, I welcome it. It makes me feel like I'm part of something important. Like my life has purpose again.

Willow is checking out the only picture with people in the room when I return to the sitting area. She leans over to see it better, and I drag my eyes away from her curvy ass just before she turns around. I place the beers on the table and watch her walk over. She looks striking in an ivory knitted dress that reaches all the way to her feet. The soft wool molds her rounded breasts and thighs and is a beautiful contrast to the silky, black waves of hair bouncing past her shoulders.

"That's a lovely family picture? Is that your brother? Was he in the military with you? You and your sisters look so young."

I down half of my bottle. I'm not used to talking about my life like this, but it's natural that Willow has questions about me. In order to give this marriage a good go, I'm going to have to open up about some things in my life.

"That was taken about ten years ago. I must have been around thirty-one. That is Danny. He was the Walters' only son. We were more like brothers of the heart. That's what he used to say anyway, after he brought me here to meet his family. He died in Afghanistan during a military operation." I trail my fingers across the side of the bottle and watch the moisture there as it drips onto my jeans.

"I'm sorry. I didn't mean to bring up terrible memories." There's compassion in Willow's eyes.

"It's been a while." But I missed him every day. I missed the loss of his dreams. Danny was only a few months away from leaving the military. He'd dreamed of running a small farm back home in Blossom Ford with a girl and a bunch of kids.

"It looks like you cared for him a lot. You were all so loving at the registry office that even though you were the only dark-haired and eyed person in the family, I thought you were blood related."

"Danny's sisters and parents are like that. The day that photo was taken was the first time I ever felt like I was part of a family. It was also my first time visiting the Walters and Blossom Ford. I came another two times with Danny and fell in love with these mountains. I joined the army straight out of high school. When I retired three years ago, I settled here." Somehow, doing some things my friend had wanted to do felt like Danny was doing them. It was a small way to give back to Danny the friendship he'd shared with me.

That's why when Mary-Jayne, Danny's youngest sister, told me I had thirty minutes to meet the bride I knew nothing about, I didn't kill her. She registered me at Blossom Ford Matchmaking Agency and responded to Willow's queries, all without my knowledge.

She looked so much like Danny when she explained I'd never have accepted to register for the agency and the reason she'd given me brief notice was because she knew that even though I didn't consider myself a gentleman; I wasn't callous enough to stand up a young woman who believed she'd met her perfect husband without an explanation.

Although I'd been mad with her, the pleading look in her blue eyes, so much like Danny's when I found out he'd sent my amateur photos to a nature magazine without my consent, eased my anger.

It also helped that the moment I saw Willow's curvy figure and the haunted look in her coffee brown eyes, I knew I'd go ahead with the arranged marriage.

Willow stares at me like she wants to ask something, but shakes her head. She takes a long sip of her beer. "I know what it's like to have a family of the heart. My friend Angel and my co-workers at Day care are like that. Especially Angel. She's like a sister, or what I imagine a sister would be like. Her granny, you saw her at the registry office, treats Jordan as if he were her great grandkid. It's the first time Jordan and I have felt welcomed as part of a family."

She blinks and turns away, but isn't fast enough for my trained eyes. I spotted tears in her eyes before she blinked.

"Mr. Clark threatened to kill me if I mistreated you."

"What? Angel's dad?"

I nod. It's not something I ever intended telling her, but those tears got me thinking she might find comfort from hearing this.

"What did he say?" The tears are back, but funnily enough, she's smiling too.

"He got close and looked me straight in the eyes." I've never been good at acting, but I change my voice. "Son, you look like someone who can use his fists and a gun, but if you hurt Willow, I'll find a way to kill you."

She giggles.

I don't know if she's laughing at my weird acting, but I feel myself smile. Her coffee brown eyes are full of mirth and her even white teeth shine against the nude gloss on her lips. She crosses both her legs under her and faces me fully.

"He must have looked a sight. I'm so sorry."

"You don't look it."

She claps a hand over her mouth as if to hide her laughter.

"I was touched, actually. It's the first time anyone ever said those words to me. It made me feel like part of a family, too."

"Thank you for telling me."

I'm wondering if she spotted the red in my cheeks.

She also plays with the condensation on her beer bottle. "I had a couple of foster parents, but mostly I grew up in group homes. I didn't click anywhere, so I don't really have a family. It's nice to know Angel's dad watched out for me like that."

All she told me about Jordan's father was that he was abusive and she was running from him. I don't think she's ready to talk about that, so I don't ask, but I know very well what it's like to be part of a family with an abusive member.

"Would you like another beer?"

She covers a yawn. "Sorry. I'm exhausted. I don't know why, it's not like there was lots to organize for the wedding. All we did was book a table at Jackson's Diner for our families."

But that wasn't all. Apart from moving their small amount of baggage, Willow had to deal with canceling her tenancy, stopping her bills and moving in with a man she hardly knew. Considering she was running away from an ex she'd once trusted; it must have taken a great deal of courage to trust another man with protecting her.

After the abuse I suffered at my father's hands and my mother's abandonment, it took me years to let Danny in and build a friendship with him. Although it wasn't the same, I was good friends with the other men I served with, so I suppose having to learn to trust the other men in my team with my safety helped me open up a little.

"Sleep with Jordan tonight."

"Are you sure?"

"We agreed to take things slow and get to know each other." I'm crazy with wanting Willow, but I don't want her sleeping with me because she's grateful. Also, although she doesn't seem bothered by my scar — apart from the initial surprise when we first met — I'm not crazy enough to scare her away by showing her the rest of my body. My burn scar runs the entire length of my right side.

Tonight, my cock will have to settle for my fist.

Chapter 3

Willow

I THOUGHT I'D HAVE a hard time sleeping. Before I arrived in Blossom Ford, I'd never lived in a small town. I had trouble falling asleep the first couple of days. Apart from the sound of a few animals, it's even quieter here in the woods. Add to that the fact that Ransom was sleeping in the room next door, it all made the cabin not conducive to sleeping. I remember nothing after my head hit the pillow, though, so I must have dozed off straight away. The daylight in the room wakes me up.

I remove Jordan's arm from my chest and place it against his small body. He's only five, but tries to be grown up when he's awake. His father is a selfish prick and I'm a bag of insecurities behind my tough exterior, so I don't know how he became such a wise and gentle little boy.

I kiss the honey-gold of his soft cheek; glad he could get a good night's sleep and quietly leave the bed. It's half past seven, way past my usual wake up time for work. I took a few days off day care so Jordan and I can get to know Ransom and our new home. I remember the humble expression on his face when he said he had enough money coming in from his pension and photography work for a decent living for the three of us so I could stop working if I wanted. It touched me. But the fact I was a stay at home mom was one way Luke used to insult me, even though he was the main reason I couldn't work—he'd hated me going out.

Ransom's not in the kitchen. When I enter the bathroom, the shower is damp and there is a faint citrusy scent in the air. An image of him showering enters my mind, making my core clench. I blow out air and switch on the tap. This wasn't the time to think about my hot husband. Quickly, I wash. In the bedroom, I dress, still careful not to wake Jordan, then head to the kitchen.

I open the refrigerator. It's bursting with groceries. There's a popular brand of kids' yoghurt I'm almost positive Ransom got for Jordan. I pull out eggs and bacon.

The front door opens, letting in a light breeze.

"Morning." Ransom walks in. His light brown hair is dark with damp.

The shower scene pops into my mind. I duck my head and greet the eggs. I just don't know what's gotten into me since the day I first saw Ransom. It's like my body was making up for the years it didn't get any action.

Ransom takes out two frying pans and puts them on the cooker. "I'll make some pancakes while you fry the eggs and bacon."

"I can do it all. It won't take long."

Ransom pauses in the act of opening a bag of flour. "I've never cooked with a woman before. It's one of my fantasies."

I blink. It's such an innocent fantasy. Why am I blushing? But even as the question forms in my mind, I know the answer. It's his deep voice and the way he looks at me. Steady, like he's eying me up before he takes me. I shiver.

"Are you cold?"

I shake my head. I dated Luke in high school and started living with him when we graduated and I found out I was pregnant. He's the only man I've known, and he'd stopped finding me attractive as soon as I started showing. I have little experience with men, but I'm almost sure I've interpreted the look in Ransom's clear gray eyes correctly.

His movements are sure as he breaks eggs and whips batter. His hands are large, like everything about him. I first noticed the burn mark on his right hand at the registry office when he put a ring on my finger. For the first time, I realize he always has his unburned side to me. Is he conscious about his scar? And does it go all the way down his body? It's too early in our relationship to ask. I understand all too well how sometimes we want to keep things to ourselves.

"How is the fantasy so far? Is it close to what you hoped for?" I tease.

"It's close. I'm enjoying it."

I toy with the desire to ask what would make it complete, as he places a perfectly browned pancake on a plate. "What's missing?"

"A back hug. That always happens in the scenes I've seen."

I stare at him. He's watching me with that intense look in his eyes again. The sizzling of oil draws my attention from him.

"I've seen that too. I've always wondered what it'd feel like. Maybe we could try it one day." I can't believe the playful voice is coming from my throat.

"I'd like that."

"How do you like your eggs?"

By the time we finish cooking, I know how Ransom likes his breakfast and what his favorite food is. And he knows mine and Jordan's too.

The knowledge brings about a strange feeling in me. It's been a long time since a man has shown interest in me.

"Mommy," a bleary-eyed Jordan calls out.

I place the plate I'm holding on the table and hug my little boy.

"Morning Jordan," Ransom says from the stove.

Jordan watches him for a while before he answers. My heart goes out to him. It took me a while to figure out that not answering people immediately was one way Jordan tests people. His dad lashed out if he didn't answer straight away.

Jordan's eyes go to the birdcage in one corner of the room. There's a tiny sparrow there.

"His name is Muller. He hurt one of his wings. We'll release him once he's better. Would you like to feed him?" Ransom asks.

Jordan nods.

"Get dressed. I'll show you how after breakfast."

Warmth fills my heart and I throw Ransom a look of gratitude.

Chapter 4

Ransom

"YOU WEREN'T KIDDING WHEN you said it was colder up here," Willow says as we head away from the cabin.

Even though it's the beginning of spring and down the mountain it's already noticeably warmer, it's still cold up here. Willow looks cute in one of my woolen hats.

"Are you warm enough?" I ask.

She points to the thick scarf around her head, which Danny's mom knitted for me. She faces the sky with widespread arms and closes her eyes.

"It feels great to be out here. I can smell the fresh, crispy air."

"It's one thing I love about living here."

I watch Jordan as he chases a squirrel until it disappears into the thick branches of a tree.

"I'd always thought I was a city girl, but I can see myself living here. Especially since you have electricity and running water."

I chuckle. It sounds strange to my ears. After Danny left, it was hard for my teammates and me to laugh. When I suffered burns during another explosion on the day I finished my service and was due to fly home, it became even harder.

"You have a delightful laugh. You should do it more often."

I can feel myself blushing. Fuck it, I'm like a teenager on his first date. It's Willow. Yesterday, she made me smile. Today, she's making me laugh.

To hide my embarrassment, I march over to Jordan, who's still staring up at the tree. I peer up and my breath catches. The squirrel is looking down at us. He looks magnificent, with the branches stretching high above him.

Quietly, so I don't scare it away, I reach for my camera. I capture the scenery before the little animal bolts.

"Can I see?" Jordan asks.

I squat. We both look at the image on the screen.

"Its eyes are huge," Jordan says, awe in his voice.

"It's a beautiful picture!" Willow exclaims beside us.

I nod.

"Will you submit it to a magazine? How much do you get for a photo like this?" she asks.

I shrug. "Depends. Anything from a couple of hundred to a couple of thousand bucks, depending on who's buying."

"Isn't it a cool job Mommy? Can I do it when I grow up? I'd get to take photos of animals and plants all day!"

I chuckle. "It's an awesome job."

We walk for about an hour and stop a few times to take pictures of animals and interesting plants, and for me to point out the nearest house, which is about half an hour away from ours. Calling the cabin ours feels strange but good. Willow and Jordan have been here for less than twenty-four hours and already, I'm feeling like we're a family.

We spend the day playing games and watching kids' programs on TV until it's Jordan's bedtime.

"Mom, can Uncle Ransom read my bedtime story?"

I led teams of men and carried out complex operations during my military service, but the fear I feel that I'll disappoint Jordan is something I've never experienced.

When he falls asleep after only a few sentences, I glance at Willow. "Is he supposed to fall asleep this quickly? I tried to change the tone of my voice to make the story more interesting, but maybe I made it sound boring."

"You were perfect," she whispers. "He's usually asleep by this time. The walk must have tired him out as well."

We watch a documentary on the geographical channel. Despite what I said yesterday, I offer to let her watch the drama we started yesterday.

"It's your turn with the remote, remember?"

Once again, being so close to Willow makes it hard to focus. I can smell the shower gel and perfume she used. I don't even know what it is exactly, but its scent is driving me wild.

When she says goodnight, I'm not sure whether to be relieved or happy. But then she leans across me and kisses my cheek. It's an innocent peck, yet my whole body goes on alert. I stare at Willow's soft lips.

Her tongue darts out of her mouth, and she licks those luscious lips. Even though I promised myself I'd take things slow with her, I can't stop myself from rubbing my thumb across her wet lip. A couple of beats pass, then she sucks my thumb.

Groaning, I snake my hand across her nape and pull her towards me. An inch away from her parted lips, I pause. When she doesn't pull away, I kiss her. Deeply, like a man who's been starved of water for too long. She kisses me back, her tongue dueling with mine as if she's just as ravenous as I am.

I angle her head for a deeper kiss. My hands rove over the swell of her breasts. She moans and my sanity returns.

I put my head against hers. "We're supposed to be taking this slow. Are you okay?"

"Yes," she whispers against my mouth.

My cock hardens. I pull away. "Goodnight Willow." I scoot as far away as I can to avoid touching her again.

Chapter 5
Willow

IT'S BEEN TWO WEEKS since I married Ransom. I've been back at work for a week and today, I'm on duty in the baby room. I change a nappy, crooning to the little girl. This is the best part of childhood. I could spend the whole day with the babies in here and still be smiling at the end of my shift.

I hope Ransom wants children because I'd like Jordan to have brothers and sisters. Thinking about babies makes me think about kissing Ransom.

We've kissed every single night since that first time. But that's all we've done. I'm so frustrated, I spend every free moment thinking about whether to tell Ransom it's time to move to the next base or, better still, the last base.

But what if my body repulses him? Luke used to say looking at me made him lose his erection. What if Ransom feels the same way?

I've never been dainty. I've always been big boned. Being five feet eight didn't help. Boys had never really wanted to talk to me.

So, when the best-looking boy at school showed interest, I was overjoyed. I was okay with my body, but the foster system had thrown me a few curve balls, so my self-esteem wasn't exactly high. I fell for Luke's easy charm and looks. Believing he loved me, I gave myself to him.

Soon after graduation, I started showing and putting on weight. That's when I noticed Luke change. He became verbally and physically abusive. My body became a turn off. After Jordan was born, I tried everything to lose weight, but nothing helped. Luke didn't want me anymore, but he wouldn't let me leave either. As his behavior worsened, so did my self-confidence.

Being away from him helped. So did having friends like Angel, who was curvy too and loved her body. I desperately want to be with Ransom, but it isn't easy to get rid of the worry he might not like my body.

Every weekday, he drives Jordan and me to daycare and picks us up. There's no bus that goes up the mountain, so I'm grateful he's happy to drive us. We spend our evenings in front of the fire, watching TV, reading or playing games.

The door to the nursery opens. Angel sticks her head round.

I rush over and hug her. "It's so nice to see you. Are you popping in to visit?"

"Yes. Oh, I've missed this room."

I chuckle. "Really? Have you been sending Liv and Ollie to your mom's?"

Angel laughs too. "I don't have to. Mom and Grannie turn up all the time. They spoil the twins so much, those adorable brats are quite happy to go off with their grandparents and great gran whenever they get the chance. But how are you?"

Angel stands in front of me and I feel like I'm on display for her. "Stop that already. I'm fine."

Angel shakes her head. "We haven't really talked about your wedding. Before you told me you were getting married, I knew you'd met someone. You've had that look of someone who's in love for a while now."

"Love? Just because you and Liam are head over heels with each other, you're seeing the l word everywhere, right?."

Angel pats a baby that's stirring. She lowers her voice. "You deserve to be happy. I think you and Ransom make a lovely couple. So, how are things really going?"

"We're taking it easy."

"Yeah? And how is that going?"

"He's kind and wonderful with Jordan. I feel like I've won the lottery."

"Why were you frowning, then?"

"I was?"

"What's the matter?"

Would Angel understand? "I'm worried Ransom might not like me."

Angel looks blank.

"All of me." I point at my body.

"Willow, some men like curvy women. Actually, a lot of the men in Blossom Ford. I don't think he would have married you if he weren't attracted to you. Besides, the way he looked at you during your wedding, he's into you."

As Angel says goodbye, I fervently hope she's right. Because I really like Ransom and want to spend the rest of my life with him. I like the way he cares for me and Jordan and his fairness and honesty. I like our quiet life and have fallen completely in love with his wooden cabin and the woods surrounding it. It feels like home.

I'm not the type to hold things in for long. After losing my fighting spirit when I was with Luke, I let him hurt me until he hit Jordan. That's when I woke up from the nightmare I'd been living in. I'd tried to get away from him before without success, but seeing my son hurt gave me the determination I needed to finally run from him successfully.

I'm done with not speaking up for myself. Tonight, I'll let Ransom know I'm ready to go all the way with him. What happens next will be up to him.

Chapter 6

Ransom

THERE'S SOMETHING DIFFERENT about Willow. I notice it the moment I set eyes on her. I open the door for Jordan and make sure his seatbelt is tucked in properly.

"Is everything alright?" I ask as I drive up the mountain.

She tells me about Angel's visit and Jordan pipes in about his day, but I still can't work out what's wrong.

The moment I park the car in front of the cabin, I know there's an intruder inside. The door isn't properly shut. Near the steps, there's a dent against the wall, like someone swung a bat at it.

"Wait Jordan," I stop the little boy as he's about to open the door. I turn to Willow. "Stay in the car. Call the cops, there's someone in the house," I whisper to her.

Her eyes widen. She frantically searches the cabin, then looks at Jordan.

I switch off the headlights.

"Don't leave the car. Lock the doors as soon as I go out."

"Where are you going? Shouldn't we head back to town?"

"Willow, trust me. It'll be fine. Sit in the back with Jordan and call the cops. Remember, I'm good at protecting people?"

She nods and scrambles to the back as I leave the car.

I lean casually against the door of the truck and check the CCTV app on my phone. There are three men. I fast forward to see if any of them came out, but they all remained inside.

They're armed with baseball bats. I slide my cell phone into my back pocket and fish out my keys, whistling.

The porch lights switch on as I climb the stairs. I insert my key into the keyhole and pretend to be surprised when the door swings back. I remove my phone and turn on the flashlight. As soon as I enter the cabin, a bat swings at me. Easily, I avoid it. I don't take any chances and quickly neutralize the untrained men inside, striking in the right places to make them unconscious. I switch on the light, then get rope from a cupboard in the kitchen area and tie them up, making sure the knots are tight.

I call Willow. Even over the phone, I can hear the terror in her voice as she asks if I'm okay.

"I tied the intruders up, but it's best if I'm here with them. Stay in the car until the cops arrive."

"Is it Luke?"

One man is identical to the photo Willow showed me of Jordan's father. "Yes."

A sigh. "Be careful."

I hang up the phone as Luke spews a string of curses. "Son of a bitch. Untie me. Do you know who my father is?"

"He's running for mayor. Has a pretty good chance of winning."

Apprehension enters Luke's eyes.

"I have a few contacts of my own. I can ensure the CCTV footage of you and your friends damaging, breaking and entering my property gets released to the opposition and the press. How would your father feel about that?"

"You're bullshitting. Do you think I'm stupid? I looked around before I came in. There were no cameras."

I press play on my cell and turn the screen to Luke. One of his friends wakes up and starts crying when he sees himself on my cell. The footage is of the best quality. The faces are clearly visible.

I stop the video.

"I recorded our conversation as well," I add. Sirens sound in the distance.

Luke and the conscious man contort themselves, trying to break free of the ropes.

"If you ever come crawling back here, you'll regret it. Willow's no longer alone. You won't be able to hurt her or Jordan anymore. Keep your mouth shut as you leave." I say in my coldest voice. I don't feel any remorse as Luke soils his pants. Bullies like him pretend to be strong until they meet someone they can't handle.

I give a concise statement to the cops and step outside before the officers are ready to leave. I don't want Jordan to see his father, especially in the state he's in.

The little boy is crying when I open the door. Willow is trying to comfort him. She's holding back tears, but I can see she won't last much longer.

"Look at him," I whisper into Willow's ear. "He won't ever hurt you again."

She looks out of the window and her mouth falls open. Luke's no longer trussed up like a chicken but is in handcuffs, yet there's no disguising his soiled trousers and the beaten air about him. I hope seeing him like that will help lessen the fear Willow has of Luke.

"Did he soil himself?" She whispers back.

I nod.

She blinks back tears. Admiration replaces the fear. "What did you do to him?"

"I threatened him with CCTV footage of him entering and breaking. His father is running for mayor. He'd love to have that scandal about his son ruin his campaign."

"He's always feared his father. That's one reason he didn't marry me. They didn't approve of me."

"It's their loss, Willow."

She nods.

"Mommy? Is daddy here?"

My heart constricts. How could a father terrify his little boy like this? Is that what I looked like when I was Jordan's age? Jordan has a fierce mom protecting him. By the time I turned five, my mom had fled.

"Jordan, it was a bear," I say and ruffle his hair.

His eyes round, just like Willow's. "Look at me. I'm okay. I took care of the bear and saved your mom and you."

He sniffles.

"For a long time, my job was protecting people. Your dad will never hurt you or your mom again. Because I'm here to make sure you're both safe. Okay?"

He nods.

"Stay here a little longer. I'm going to clean the house."

Chapter 7

Willow

WE FINALLY GOT Jordan to sleep. In the sitting room, I wrap my arms around Ransom and listen to the crackling of the fire. His arms tighten around me and I finally feel safe.

"You ate little. Do you want a snack?"

I shake my head. Now, more than before, I want no more uncertainties between us. "I've been thinking about something the past few days."

"What is it?"

"I'm ready to go all the way. If you'll have me, I want to be your true wife. How do you feel about it?"

He coughs. Clears his throat.

"Are you saying that because of what happened tonight? I don't want you to give yourself to me out of gratitude."

I shift around on the sofa until I'm straddling him and touching both of his cheeks, the scarred and the good. "I'm falling in love with you. The fact you can protect me and Jordan is part of the reason. But it's not the only reason. I've been feeling like this for the past few days. I love the way you make me feel like a queen. The way you care for the injured animals in the woods warms me up. I'm falling for you because you're you, Ransom."

I frown. "Actually, I fell in lust with you the first time I saw you in town, a little while before I joined the matchmaking agency. I'd think of you when I touched myself."

He blinks twice, then picks me up and deposits me on the bed in his bedroom. He goes to the wall, switches on the light and then comes and stands by the bed. Slowly, he undresses until he's standing naked before me.

I get up and touch the burned skin down the right side of his torso and hip. It's darker and rougher than the left-hand side of his body. I put my lips where my hands touch and kiss down his chest, on both sides. I can feel my panties getting wet.

I touch his cock. He's large there as well. I lick my lips, wondering if he'd fit inside my mouth. I kneel in front of him, but Ransom stops me with a strangled cry and hands on my shoulders.

"What's the matter?" I ask, staring at his engorged shaft as it stretches towards my lips.

When he doesn't answer, I look up. He's wiping tears.

I freeze.

"Did I hurt you?"

He lifts me up. His shoulders shake and I realize he's laughing.

"I bloody love you, Willow." His lips crush down on mine. He rips my top and pulls down my pants.

I cover my tummy. Of all my bits, that's the part of me Luke hated the most. "The lights." I want to hide under the covers but am worried about my tummy being on display as I dash to the bed.

"You're stunning, Willow. Let me see all of you, like you did with me."

Gently, he pulls my hands away.

"Look at me," Ransom commands. "See how I'm dying for you?"

Sure enough, his cock is still standing proud, larger than it was.

He takes my hand and rubs it up and down his shaft.

Moisture seeps down my thigh. I'm so turned on right now.

"Make love to me, Ransom," I plead.

He pushes me on the bed and inserts a finger into me.

"God, Willow, you're ready for me. I wanted our first time to be crazy good for you. I don't think I can last long enough." His words are breathy on my nipple.

I bend my knees and guide him into me. I breathe against the burn as Ransom inches into me. He grabs my cheeks and kisses me until he's all the way in.

"Are you okay?" He rasps against my lips.

My hands are damp from the sweat on his back.

I squeeze my core. Ransom sets a fast-paced rhythm and I meet his every stroke, glad to at last be his. His lips graze my neck, biting lightly. I moan.

He slides a hand between us and rubs my clit. I come apart, my body arching under him as pleasure shoots into every corner of my body.

He shouts my name and bucks into me until he's spent.

I must have fallen asleep because when I open my eyes, I'm lying on Ransom's chest.

"We didn't wake up Jordan?"

"It's a little late to worry about that, sleepyhead." He brushes my hair away from my face. "I checked on him. He's fast asleep."

"Did I tell you I love you?"

"I'll never tire of hearing it. Poor Jordan, he's going to get so much love from me."

I chuckle. I love hearing Ransom joke.

He bites my neck. I shiver.

"You like this." His hands cup my ass and knead it. I like that too, I realize. I wriggle until I come into contact with his semi-hard shaft.

"I like this too." I stroke up and down him. He must have cleaned us up because only the crown is wet. Pleasure fills me when I realize I'm making Ransom hard.

There's so much I like about him. Tears of happiness fill my eyes as I realize we have a lifetime to discover together what makes us both happy.

Epilogue

Ransom

Three years later

I'M SPEEDING, BUT THERE's no way I can drive slower. My heart is so fucking tight, it hurts to breathe. I park outside the emergency department of Weston-Parker General Hospital and rush inside.

"My wife was brought in a while ago," I say to the receptionist.

I follow the directions the man provides after I give Willow's name.

Willow is sleeping when I get to her side.

A doctor comes over as I take her hand.

"I'm her husband," I say. "What's wrong with her?"

"I'm Dr. Jamal Stone. Your wife has acute indigestion."

Willow wakes up, squeezes my hand.

"Hi Jamal," she says to the doctor.

"Willow. How are you feeling?"

Willow introduces us first. Jamal is Angel's husband's colleague and friend.

"The pain is gone." She frowns. "It was severe before. I couldn't breathe."

"That's how acute indigestion works."

"I've never had it," Willow says. "Why now?"

The doctor looks at us, then smiles. "I guess you didn't know. Congratulations, you're pregnant."

I look at Willow. My chest is tight again, but it's a different tightness. We wanted a baby early in our marriage and hadn't been successful. I'd started thinking that maybe it would not happen.

"Pregnancy can cause indigestion. Always carry some medicine with you. It was nice seeing you." The doctor heads toward the nurses' station.

Willow's hand tightens in mine.

"Jordan is going to have a baby brother or sister," I say.

Tears stream down her face. "I wonder if that's why I've been so emotional. I've also put on some weight."

I laugh. "I'll love every part of you."

"We're in a hospital, big man."

She hasn't stopped calling me that since she discovered how much I love it.

"Alright, sweetheart."

I can't wait to have another child with Willow. After realizing I'd be nothing like my dad, I've become more confident in taking care of Jordan. I love being his dad.

Every day, it becomes a little easier to speak about the wounds of my past and I thank God Willow came into my life.

MARRYING THE OBSESSED CEO

CURVY BRIDES OF BLOSSOM FORD BOOK 7

IRIS WEST

Chapter 1
Winona

"I'M GOING TO HAVE a fantastic day! My colleagues will be wonderful people. There won't be anything I can't solve," I whisper to myself as I stroll towards my new job at Sanders Solutions, one of the fastest growing management consultancy firms in the country.

The nerves don't vanish, but visualizing a good day and repeating positive affirmations makes me feel a little better. It helps that even though it's just gone seven, and it's late February, the sun is shining, and the air is pleasantly warm. Best of all, the cramps and migraine that had me bedridden yesterday are completely gone. If my period had started today, I would have had to call in sick on my first day, which would have sucked. I'm taking coming on yesterday as a good omen that this is going to be a great day.

I need this job to be a success to prove to myself that moving back home to Blossom Ford isn't a complete failure. Otherwise, I'll be forced to accept the fact that I couldn't stomach living away from home when I insisted on living in Boston after college and graduate school, instead of bowing down to fate and doing what's expected of me; working for Blossom Ford Matchmaking Agency, like all the eldest girls of my family have done for generations.

Even though I missed home like crazy, I only left my job of one year at a large Boston firm when I found something better at home. My post at Sanders Solution is initially for a four-month maternity cover and the company is not as large as the top firm I worked for in Boston, still it comes with the possibility of permanent employment if I prove myself as assistant to the CEO, plus it's a promotion with better pay and performance bonuses.

I have my own apartment, which means I'm independent. Popping home nearly every day and sleeping over at weekends doesn't count as being too reliant on my family's company, it just shows I missed them when I lived away.

Besides, in a couple of weeks, Mom and Dad are going to visit one of my uncles who's been ill for a while. I'm learning to manage the agency so I can resolve any issues if anything urgent comes up. That's easier done at home. If I need any files, I can slip into the agency's small office, which is next to our house.

If only I could get my love life or lack of sorted, I'd be on cloud nine. Honestly, what twenty-five-year-old girl hasn't had at least one serious relationship? The type where one considers marriage or living together. The feeling that I'm the only one just won't go away. It's not that I'm not trying. The last three years I've been on countless dates, but they led nowhere. The men are too tall or short, too talkative or quiet, etc. My brain and body have come up with many excuses for why my dates weren't worth second chances.

And it's all because of one man. My one-night stand of three years ago. I don't even know his name, so I call him Lothario, but I remember his mesmerizing cerulean blue eyes and the feel of his beard and calloused hands on my feverish skin. I can't forget his chiseled face because I dream of him almost every night. Vivid dreams that leave me panting, my pussy wet, when I wake up.

I don't know what to do to forget him. I definitely can't forget how gentle he became when he realized I was a virgin and the tender way he wiped the blood off my thighs afterward.

My friends and I had flown to New York City from Boston for a weekend trip and when we hit the bar, they dared me to lose my virginity. They'd tried the dare countless times before, but I'd never given in. Yet, that night, from the moment I saw Lothario, I was powerless against the lust that surged within me.

I greet the two security men at the entrance of the building that houses my new company. Fishing out my badge, I let myself in and take the elevator to the top of the building. Sanders Solutions occupies the top two floors, with the executives being on the fifteenth floor.

I pass quiet desks and offices until I reach my room. Light peeps through the door of the CEO's office and my lips quirk up.

It's not even half past seven. I feel sorry for his private life, but I love his dedication to work. No wonder he made the company he started in college into the giant force it is today in only fifteen years.

Julian Sanders was a lost, hurting young man when I tried to comfort him seventeen years ago. Aged eight, I'd been mad at having to attend a funeral where I was the only child. I was bored and was exploring the Sanders' small house when I stumbled on him inside his deceased grandad's bedroom. He'd looked old to me, but now I know he must have been around twenty-three, and although I couldn't really explain the depth of the feelings his naked eyes conveyed, I'd felt like he was the saddest person in the world.

When I told Mom the name of the company I'd be working for, she'd explained it belonged to Mr. Sanders' grandson. I can't wait to meet him.

Few people had a good word to say about him during the two years he lived in Blossom Ford when he was a teenager. He'd dropped out of high school and run off to a big city and only visited his grandad on Christmas day.

But now he was back in town as a highly respected owner of a business that generated billions in revenue and created jobs in town.

I slide out of my sneakers and slip into my favorite work heels. I switch on my laptop and once again go over the notes from Mr. Sanders' assistant, whom I was supposed to shadow for a few days. She went into early labor but left a comprehensive itemized list of instructions.

Eager to start my day and meet my new boss, I head to his office.

"Come in," a deep voice calls out in reply to my knock.

A shiver runs up my spine. I know that voice. Intimately. It whispers to me in the dark of night and sometimes when I'm showering.

I shake my head. Remind myself this is a place of work. Lothario and the delicious things he does to me don't belong here.

I square my shoulders, lift my chin and open the door.

Julian Sanders is staring at the screen of one of the laptops on his massive desk. He looks up and the greeting at the tip of my mouth vanishes.

Familiar blue eyes under thick chestnut brows root me to the spot. It's Lothario! His hair is cropped shorter at the sides and his beard is thicker, but his wide forehead and crooked nose remain the same. A dark tailored suit jacket encases his broad shoulders, just like that fateful night in New York City three years ago.

I blink, twice. Lothario is still watching me. It's hard to tell if he remembers me, but the fire in his eyes is unmistakable. It makes me feel owned, as if he branded me. Heat suffuses my whole body and face. Desire stirs my core. A part of my mind wonders if that look is the reason I could not forget this man.

The sound of voices, probably from the cleaning crew, brings me back to my senses.

I remind myself that I need this job. The precious pleasure this man brought me belongs only in the deepest recesses of my mind. The only thing I can do in this situation is to behave as the professional I'm supposed to be. Because Lothario is my boss, and that means nothing can ever happen between the two of us.

Once again, I set my shoulders back and lift my chin. My mouth is dry, so I clear my throat and march forward.

"Good morning Mr. Sanders. It's a pleasure to meet you. I'm Winona Smith, your temporary assistant." I stretch my hand out, glad I learned to fake a smile and a firm voice like a pro.

Chapter 2
Julian

I STAND UP AND clutch Winona's, not Temptress as I call her in my dreams, hand. It's soft and plump, just like her. Her nails are red gold and clipped short like they were that night.

I hold on a little longer than necessary but when I speak, my voice hides the bottomless cauldron of frustration and raging need this beauty has caused inside me since I met her three long years ago. I tried meeting the most beautiful women on the planet and working myself to exhaustion in order to forget her, to no avail. She's an obsession I can't rid myself of.

"Julian Sanders. The pleasure is all mine."

This expression has never made more sense than it does at this moment. My mind is stuck on the word mine like a broken record. And it's been playing since the moment I looked up and saw her.

I've been dreaming of this woman practically every time I close my eyes. Her peaches and cream scent, the taste of her rosy lips, the way her tightly curled hair feels in my hands, and the screams she makes when she comes are imprinted in my mind. So is the smile that lights up her champagne hued eyes and the so right way she felt as she slept in my arms.

She's still as alluring and sexy as I remember. But there's a deeper level of maturity and confidence about her eyes that wasn't there before. I've felt lust and a sense of belonging for my temptress, but now respect and pride warm my heart at the way she's holding herself straight, her chin jutting forward.

I spied the shock on her face when she saw me. She recognized me. I don't know how much of an impression I made in her life, but it's clear she hasn't forgotten our heated night of passion. The blush on her cheeks may be a sign of embarrassment, however, the heat in her eyes tells me she still finds me attractive.

That and the determination in her posture calm the urge to splay her over my desk and make love to her body until she's senseless with pleasure.

I am not an animal, no matter how I feel like one right now.

The cool tone of her voice reminds me of my responsibilities as her employer. I motion for her to sit and silently say a thank you because I'm wearing my suit jacket so she's not embarrassed by my hard on.

"Did you bring yourself up to speed with the status of our most pressing projects and what needs organizing the next couple of days?" My voice is rougher than usual, yet there's nothing I can do about it. It's taken everything in me to control myself and pretend this is the first time we're meeting and my hands are not dying to touch her.

I don't give a fuck what people think of me, but I want her to like me. For now, I'll go along with pretending like we're strangers, like she apparently wants.

"Yes. I've organized the notes for the two conference calls this afternoon. I'll contact our new client and make an initial assessment on the implementation of the new audible software."

We spend the next half-hour going over the most complex of our current projects.

"I'm impressed. Lori was on point when she said you're going to be one of her best hires. Welcome to Sanders Solutions."

My assistant wasn't easily impressed, but she raved about Winona's analytical, planning and problem-solving skills. I'd been a little skeptical because although Winona earned her MBA summa cum laude, her working experience was limited to a year of full-time employment, albeit with one of the best management consultancy firms in the world, and internships she'd taken over the summer breaks of her college life. Thank God I trusted my employees' judgement and Winona was hired.

"Thank you. Would you like a cup of coffee?"

It's a perfectly normal question, and her voice is only projecting politeness. Why is my mind suddenly filled with images of the flirty way she'd approached me at the bar in New York?

I don't need a drink, but I want to see her walk toward me again, so I nod and watch the sway of her hips until she leaves the room.

I erupt out of my chair and face the stretch of mountain visible through the floor to ceiling glass walls. It's a breathtaking view, but today, there's too much chaos in my mind for me to enjoy it.

Fucking hell!

I searched for Winona after she snuck out of our hotel room. I returned to the bar I met her again and again, hoping to find her there. Every time I saw a curvy, caramel skinned woman, my hopes would rise only to be crushed when they turned out to be someone else. There's no way I can accept just being colleagues with her.

I won't break my rule of not getting involved with the staff. I solve problems for a living. Somehow, I'll have to solve this one too.

I shove my hands into my trousers' pockets and pace across the length of the office. In the last couple of months, I've been thinking about creating a foundation to fund facilities that provide respite care for parents of disabled children. It's an idea that was put forward by one of my employees who has a disabled nephew. He'd been passionate when he talked about the toll caring for the disabled child took, but his field of expertise lies in computer programming.

Maybe it's something Winona can manage when Lori returns from maternity leave. She'd shown an interest in staying with the company once her initial four months were up.

I stop myself.

What the hell am I doing?

I don't even know what the woman wants. Over the years, I've wondered about why she scurried out of the hotel suite without so much as a goodbye. She'd enjoyed the sex as much as I did. Although she'd been experienced at flirting and foreplay, the red stains on her thighs and sheet proved this wasn't something she did often.

A lot of reasons popped into my mind. Ultimately, I used my experience to conclude that although she'd loved the sex, our time together hadn't meant more to her than the desire to scratch an itch. Although unexpected, it had meant so much more to me.

Before Winona, sex was a way to blow off steam from a hard day of work. I made sure my partners knew it. The idea of having the same sexual partner for a long period was burdensome.

Now, I want Winona in my life. If she's married, I won't touch her. But anything else, I'm ready to deal with. I'll do whatever it takes to make her realize she'll have a better life with me.

Chapter 3
Winona

IT'S MY THIRD DAY at Sanders Solutions and I'm exhausted. I've been attending meetings, introducing myself to clients and working on some complex projects the company has taken on, as well as getting to know the other staff members. It's better this way because during work hours, I have very little time to think about how Lothario has only become hotter and harder to resist.

He insists I call him Julian. Since everyone seems to be on a first name basis, I cave in.

A problem arises with one of our clients, so we stay later than usual. There are about ten of us in the meeting room and we eat takeout pizza as we work to clear the issue. By half-past nine, most of the work is done and only Julian and I remain to tidy things up.

"We're done. I'll give you a lift." Julian stands up and rotates his shoulders.

"You don't have to. It's late, you should get some rest."

He fixes those irresistible blues on me. "I think you have the wrong idea about me."

His tone is light. His lips quirk up just the tiniest bit as he affects a hurt expression.

I've seen his sexy, dominant, hard-working, serious and generous sides, but this is the first time he's shown his playful side in front of me. Even when we flirted in the past, he was guarded.

My lips lift in response.

"I took Lori home occasionally. It's late. I've seen you walk in the morning, so I know you are not driving. Is it wrong of me to want to do the gentlemanly thing and offer you a ride?"

Now I feel petty.

"I'll get my things."

We both grab our stuff and head for the elevator. The moment the door closes on us, I become super aware of Julian. His scent, a combination of musk and something that's just him, reaches my nostrils. It's like a drug to me. Suddenly, the taste of his kiss and the seductive warmth of his touch against my skin rush to my mind and I'm reminded of the reason I didn't want to take him up on his offer of a ride. Being alone with him in such a close space is sweet torture. I want to touch him but can't.

In his car, I sink into the luxurious passenger seat and almost purr at how comfortable I feel. He asks for my address and heads off the minute I finish speaking.

"How did you start your business?" I ask. I'm curious, but I also need something to focus on other than the confident way his powerful hands move over the wheel.

"Through sheer desperation." He glances at me.

I'm even more curious now.

"I'm a high school dropout. I blamed my unhappy childhood for everything that went wrong in my life and wanted to get back at the world that didn't seem to give a damn about me. I wasted my late teens and early twenties drinking away every penny I made."

He stops at a red light and stares at me. I gaze back at him, surprised by his expression and the way he's willing to open himself up. His employees admire and respect him, but they all seem to have the impression that he keeps his private life to himself. He was never this open three years ago.

"Then one day I was truly alone, I realized I had to change."

He gives me a lopsided grin.

"A little angel told me I was a good boy."

"An angel?"

"A know it all of a little girl. She gave me a rainbow lollipop too. Said it'd give me a little happiness."

I choke.

"Okay?" Concern lines his face.

I nod. I don't know whether to tell him I'm that little girl. This is so messed up. I want to tell him I'm touched he remembers something that happened all those years ago and that my words actually comforted him. But the one-night incident, the best and worst decision of my life, makes me unsure.

Julian pulls up outside my block of flats, kills the engine, and turns to me.

"Did the lollipop bring you happiness?" He doesn't seem like the type of man to believe in childish things like that.

"She was at my grandad's funeral. He and my mom didn't get along, so I didn't meet him until I was fourteen, when he had to take me in. I was dealing with my own demons, and he wasn't much of a talker. Suddenly being responsible for a troubled teen couldn't have been easy for him, but I didn't see that."

"It must have been hard for both of you," I add. I was too young to be aware of what was happening, but I heard scraps from adults' conversation about how tough and sad things were for the Sanders.

"She, my little angel, said she'd overheard grandad say he hoped I'd realize I was a good boy and would do something with my life, when I asked how she knew what I was like."

"She was right. You are a good man. You give so much back to society, and you genuinely care about your staff."

Something shifts in his eyes. He cocks his head. There's a hint of a smile in his eyes.

"That's not what it looked like when you refused a lift."

I blink at him. "It's only a five-minute drive. I wanted to save you the trouble."

Julian is watching me so closely, as if he's trying to figure me out.

"What did you do after your encounter with your little angel?"

"I took the GED, went to college, and worked my ass off. When things got tough, I looked at the lollipop and reminded myself Grandad had believed in me. I started the company my second year of college and grew it little by little."

"You must be proud of yourself. Your grandad would be proud of you too."

A tinge of pink shades his cheeks. This time, when he smiles, his eyes crinkle and I can see his even white teeth.

"I hope so."

Warmth spreads through me and I know it's going to be almost impossible stopping the journey from lust to more. In the last three days, I've fallen a little in love with Julian's drive and passion for his work, but seeing this humble side of him just took that to another level.

"Thanks for the lift. I'll see you tomorrow."

He waits until I'm inside the building before he drives off.

Chapter 4
Julian

I WAKE UP TO a cry of pleasure and a wet, rock-hard cock. I grab onto it and stroke up and down, spreading the moisture at the tip so my hand glides over the sensitive skin. My ministrations are no-where near as good as Winona's three years ago, and the way she pleasures me in my dreams, but they'll do. After only five pumps I grunt at the feel-good sensation as semen spurts onto my stomach and navel, where the word Temptress is inked in vivid black letters.

Dreaming about that night again and again has been both pleasurable and painful. Seeing my temptress every day, working with her, is making me long for her even more.

I'm glad it's Monday. The weekend felt empty without her. I thought about making up an excuse so she'd have to work some of the weekend, but remembering the sight of her yawning at the end of a hectic Friday stopped me.

Now and then, I'd look up, expecting her to march into my office with a cup of coffee. Even though we've been working together for only a week, it felt weird not seeing her at her desk, poring over something on her laptop. I've always worked weekends and loved it when I was the only soul there, just as much as I loved being at the office with my employees working in the background.

For the first time, on a weekend, being alone at the office felt lonely.

It was a relief when seven o'clock came and I headed for the dojo and released a lot of my pent up frustration punching, striking and kicking the boxing bag.

I slide out of the massive bed and strip the sheets. As I shower and get ready for work, I think about the plan I've devised to seduce my temptress.

The file that HR has about her suggests she's single. She seems to be comfortable pretending our one night together never happened, therefore for now, I'll carry on going along with it.

When I think about the night I told Winona my story, I'm filled with embarrassment. That was the first time I'd ever told anyone about the dark and painful days of my teenage years. I've given interviews to magazines about the rise of Sanders Solutions, but I always keep the personal stuff about Grandad, Mom, and the troubled teenager I was out of it. Saying I had a tough childhood was all I'd ever been willing to say.

I wanted Winona to know where I come from. I was also hoping that opening up about myself will make her want to do the same. Already, the caution in her eyes has diminished. I'm seeing more of the friendly and flirty personality she showed that night three years ago.

Being a caring and friendly employer while creating as many opportunities as possible to spend time with her has made Winona trust me a little and is giving us a chance to get to know each other.

My house is under the mountains of Blossom Ford, so the drive to work only takes ten minutes. It's seven o'clock when I walk into the office, excited for the challenges work will bring and the anticipation of spending time with Winona.

Half an hour later, I sense her arrival. Even though she comes into the office quietly, I always know when she's around. Once she changes out of her sneakers, the staccato clicks of her heels let me know when she's approaching my office.

I must look silly with the huge grin on my face, but I don't give a toss. Work has never been so sweet.

WINONA AND I have been working in my office for a couple of hours when an employee brings a food delivery bag.

"Let's take a break," I say after the staff member leaves.

I make space on the table for the food.

"Do you need some time alone?" I ask when she gathers up her laptop and tablet.

"We've eaten together when we worked over lunch with the teams. Since it's just the two of us, I thought you might prefer to eat alone."

"I honestly think talking about something other than work for a few minutes while eating generates more creativity once the break is over. Maybe bonding over food helps people work together better. There's more than enough food for us, too."

Winona chuckles. Just listening to the sound makes me feel good. Her hair is up and she's wearing one of her belted jumpsuits, a red one this time, that flows over her curves and shows some of the skin above her cleavage. I smash that train of thought because it leads to a dangerous path.

"I think the creativity may have something to do with being grateful for a free lunch, the overtime pay and the excellent working conditions. They are great motivators for productivity."

"You got me." I watch her bite into a sandwich and focus on eating. "How was your weekend?" I ask when I finish a sandwich.

"Mom runs a small business. She's traveling in a couple of weeks, so she's been showing me the ropes so I can deal with any urgent queries that come up while she's away. I spent the weekend and last weekend working on the business on my own to make sure I don't get any surprises. I prefer to learn by practice."

"How did it go?"

"It was frustrating." She sighs. "Mom is a college graduate, but she runs the business in an old-fashioned way. She'd have more clients and be much more successful if she only changed a few things. It wouldn't take much too."

As I listen to her ideas for improving her mom's business and give a few of my own, I realize I love this side of her. The way she becomes animated when she's talking about something she's interested in.

Chapter 5

Winona

I PLACE THE BAR of chocolate Ebony, the only other staff member younger than me, gifted as my one-month employment anniversary on my desk. She's so friendly and reminds me of my best friend, Ella.

My cell vibrates. It's Shanay, Granny's caregiver. I'm about to clock out. Why is she calling? Heart sinking, I pick up.

"I'm so sorry Winona. Your granny took a nap an hour ago. I went to check in on her, but she wasn't there. I'm so sorry, but I can't find her," she sobs.

The cell slips through my fingers. I'm numb everywhere. My legs give way and I drop onto the chair behind me.

"What's the matter?" Julian asks as he comes toward me.

My mind is blank.

He picks up the phone, listens for a while.

"We'll call back in a minute," he says.

He puts his hands on my shoulders. I focus on him.

"I have a family emergency. I need to go."

"I'll give you a ride."

I call Shanay back as we head to the elevator. She's already contacted the police.

"Stay there and keep the house line open, in case someone calls with news. I'll check the places she might have gone."

"I'll call the diner. She might have gone there. Thank God the weather's warm. Should I call your mom and dad?"

"No!"

"Where to?" Julian asks.

"The main part of town. There's a park near Jackson's Diner she loves to visit. She likes the diner, too."

I blink back tears. Granny has gone missing a few times when I was away in college, but Mom and Dad always told me after they'd found her. Every time it happened, they must have felt as distressed as I am right now.

I look left and right, scanning the pavements. Mom and Dad have not found Granny on this side of town, but I might as well eliminate the area while I'm passing through.

Something warm touches my hand. It's Julian's hand. I've been clutching my bag so hard, my knuckles have turned white. I place my hands flat against the bag, and Julian threads his fingers through mine.

I squeeze his hand, grateful.

"Where else might she have gone?"

I know all the places she's been found before, but in my mind I go over the list Mom left of likely places Granny might go to.

"The cinema and the elementary school. The point too, she likes the river."

"Tell me about your granny. What's she like?"

I smile. Granny's one of my favorite people. Maybe because she's always lived with us, in some ways, I'm closer to her than Mom.

After I tell Julian about her physical appearance, I talk about learning to cook from her and going berry picking together. When I was little, if I wasn't playing with Ella, I was hanging out with Granny. Even now, when her memory of the latest part of her life is fading, she still remembers most of those moments.

She's not at Jackson's Diner or the park. Neither is she at Raven's hairdresser. We still have more places to check, and I know an officer is looking for her and word has gotten round, which means the townsfolk will keep an eye out for her, but it's hard to keep the panic away.

I'm debating where to go next when Julian stops at a traffic light and my cell rings.

"She's at the grocery store. Lucy just called," the caregiver says when I answer the phone.

I wipe away a tear and look at Julian. His face is a study in concern.

"The grocery store over there. The store owner's daughter just called."

I sprint out of the car when Julian stops the car. Granny is sitting comfortably inside the shop drinking lemonade. When I wrap her tightly in my arms, she pushes my hands away.

"What's this fuss about? I only popped out to get some popsicles. They are out of stock of my favorite brand. I'm tired. Let's go home."

I thank Lucy and walk out with Granny.

Maybe she's just realized Julian is with us because when he opens the car door for her, she freezes. She stares up at him for ages and I'm about to guide her into the car when her gaze shifts to me.

"He's a little too much like his granddaddy, but I like him. He'll be a good husband to you," she says, then gets into the car.

I am mortified. How could Granny play cupid at a moment like this? In front of Julian, of all people. That I agree with her is irrelevant right now.

"Sometimes Granny–"

"I'm glad she approves of me," Julian cuts me off.

I decide to deal with that later and get into the back of the car with Granny.

"Your Granny's house or your apartment?" Julian asks.

"Granny's. My parents are away. I'm staying there for the time being."

I call the caregiver, thank her and tell the poor woman to go home.

Chapter 6
Julian

WINONA'S GRANNY'S HOUSE HAS changed little in the last twenty years. I remember coming here a few times to run errands for Grandad. It must have been about a year before Winona was born. A thought suddenly occurs to me. What if the reason Winona left without saying goodbye that night is my age? I make sure I'm fit and healthy, but she's young. What if our age gap is a deal breaker for anything more than a one-night stand?

I get up from the sofa and stroll towards a vast frame with a collage of family photos. I recognize Winona's parents. Although I didn't know their identity, they were at Grandad's funeral. Almost in all the photos, Winona's making a funny face. I'm not even surprised when I find that cute. My brain is obsessed with anything she does.

A couple of pictures catch my attention. My angel, the little girl that spoke with me at the funeral, is in them, with Winona's granny in one and Winona's parents in another. I look back at the other photos.

Winona is my little angel!

I don't know why she didn't mention it when I told her about my past. The only way I'll know the answer is by asking, so I keep busy as I wait for her to settle her granny.

I head out of the living room and go searching for the kitchen. We left the office just after six and it's now half-past eight. Winona's probably hungry. I want to make a cup of tea or coffee; it might help if she's still in shock. Don't people on TV use hot drinks to calm others?

I'm more of a scotch type man whenever I need to calm down, and so were Mom and Grandad. I find the kettle, fill it up and switch it on. When I stand in front of the refrigerator, I'm suddenly struck with unfamiliar nerves. What if Winona's parents object to having a stranger rummaging in their refrigerator?

I shake the nerves off. I doubt Winona wants takeout. Her granny would sometimes take us food. This house seems like the type that might always have something to eat lying around. Sure enough, there's some stew inside.

I warm some up, make two cups of coffee and set them on the table, just as footsteps sound on the stairs.

"I'm in the kitchen."

"Oh," Winona says when she sees me. "I was gone so long, I thought you'd left. I was going to call."

There are tear tracks on her cheeks. I want to sit with her on my lap, pat her back and say I don't know what to comfort her. Instead, I fold my arms over my chest to stop myself from putting thought into action. We need to talk first.

"I'm going to wash my face."

Back in the kitchen, she gulps her food. "Thanks for this. I was craving Granny's food. She made it yesterday."

"It's good. I never let on, but I used to love this whenever your granny gave some to Grandad."

She's silent, her champagne eyes downcast.

"We can talk another day. I'll do the dishes and go."

She finishes her food and grabs her coffee.

"I'm a little tired, but I want to talk. What happened with Granny made me realize I've been running away from some things and it's time to stop."

"What do you mean?" It sounds like she's talking about more than us.

"Kids used to call Granny a witch. And later Mom. I think that's when I began thinking I wanted nothing to do with our centuries old matchmaking agency and our female ancestors' knowledge of medicinal herbs."

She smiles.

"I don't know if you're aware, but our matchmaking agency has only ever been run by the daughters of our family. We have a sixth sense, that I suppose some people might call intuition, for matching the right couples. I hated the expectation that as the only daughter, that's what I'd do. So, I did something else and am good at it." She takes another deep breath.

"But I've loved helping Mom run the agency the last few weeks. I want to modernize it, run it my way. And I want to spend more time with Granny while she still recognizes me. I think Mom wants that too. We can both do that if I run the agency."

I nod.

"You're not surprised?"

"When you talked about your mom's small business, I kind of figured you were in love with it."

"I'll complete my contract."

I want this woman permanently in my life. I want to marry her.

"I'm sorry I pretended not to know you. That first day at the office, I panicked. I didn't know how you'd feel about us working together. I also wasn't sure if you remembered me. Pretending we'd never met seemed to be the best option."

"I remember every single moment."

She blushes. Her tongue pops out and wets her lips. My eyes track the movement.

"Me too. It was the most amazing night of my life. You looked very successful; I didn't think you'd want to date me-"

"I dreamed about you for three years. I searched for you, too."

"I went back to Boston straight away." Her fingers play with the side of her cup. "I would have tried to persuade you, but even before we went to the hotel room, you made it clear you weren't interested in relationships."

Before I fell asleep, I should have made it clear to her that in the time we were together, I changed my mind.

"That was before you. I'm sorry I didn't clarify that before I fell asleep. Since that night, you're the only woman I've thought of. I want you in my life." I curse myself for my choice of words. Why the hell did I find it hard to talk about my personal feelings? Should I have asked her out? Like on a date?

"You don't get involved with your staff."

Is she flirting with me? My eyes narrow.

Winona smiles. I lean back on the chair.

"You're planning to leave in three months' time. Even if you weren't, I had a plan."

I tell her about my solution, and she grins.

"What did you mean by wanting me in your life?"

There's desire in her eyes, but there's something else too. In the four weeks since she began working for me, I've become familiar with the expressions that flit across her face.

"I already know I want to spend the rest of my life with you. I understand you might not feel the same yet. Will you go out with me? To find out?"

"The day I finish my contract."

We stare at each other. I've never met a woman with such a perfect combination of sass and sweetness. My heart stutters and I know I love her. I'm willing to wait for her.

"I saw your family photos; I know you're my little angel."

"Sorry about that too. I wanted to tell you; I just wasn't sure how because of the one-night stand issue."

"Promise me one thing."

"What is it?"

"Let's be open with each other about things that affect our relationship."

"Deal."

Chapter 7
Winona

IT'S MY LAST DAY at Sanders Solutions. I've said my goodbyes. It's one minute to seven o'clock, and it's Friday. It's so quiet, I think Julian and I are the only ones who haven't left.

My office phone rings.

"Miss Smith, come into my office, please."

I frown. As I walk into his room, the minute hand strikes 12. Officially, I'm no longer Julian's employee.

"Lock the door."

I shiver at the tone of his voice. I lock the door and look back at Julian. He's out of the chair and marches straight to me.

"I'm going to worship you tonight, Temptress," he whispers against my mouth.

I wrap my arms around the nape of his neck and hold on for dear life as he devours my mouth in a wet kiss that makes my knees weak.

I'm grateful when he picks me up, still kissing me. I hook my legs around him and kiss him back, abandoning myself to the pleasure coursing through my body.

He meanders to the desk and lowers me onto it. I open my legs and watch him step into the space between them.

"I love how thick your beard is."

I slide my hands up the sides of his face, delighting in the sensation of the bristles against my palms. Julian turns his head, captures one of my fingers into his mouth, and sucks on it. My core clenches.

I snake one arm round his neck and pull him down, wanting his mouth on me again. He nibbles my lower lip, draws it into his mouth with just the right amount of pressure.

He palms my breasts through the fabric of my dress, then squeezes them.

I moan into his mouth.

When I come up for air, Julian presses tiny kisses over my eyes, nose and jaw while his hands glide over my belly and thighs.

"I want to see you, Temptress."

The roughness in his voice is such a turn on.

I place my hand on the zip of my dress, but he removes it.

He drags the zip past my thighs until both sides of the dress fall open.

"I love this dress."

I lift so he can pull the dress from under me.

He removes my strapless bra and panties and stares at me, eyes darkening.

"Lie down." He shoves the papers on his desk away.

I lean back, feeling like a cat. The only other time I've ever been this exposed was the night we spent together. The heat in his eyes makes me feel wanton and takes away my shyness.

"Open your legs. I want to see the dark pink of your pussy. Stretch your arms above you."

He watches me like he's imagining the things he wants to do to me. My whole body is on fire. My chest rises with my quick breaths.

Julian strips slowly, his eyes roving over me. His large cock jerks against his stomach. My eyes widen at how aroused he is.

"You got a tattoo?" It wasn't there before.

"Keep your hands up. Don't move."

"I want to see it."

He moves his cock away and I see it. It's so sexy, moistures seeps out of me. I bite my lip.

"You're my temptress, Winona. That's what I called you, the three years I didn't know your name."

Tears fill my eyes. Julian rubs his nose up the slit of my pussy and I cry out, tears forgotten.

"I missed this scent." He kisses the inside of my thighs, then kneels on the floor and places my legs on his shoulders.

He opens me wide, licks my clit. He blows on it like he's playing with a favorite toy, takes it into his mouth and sucks repeatedly until my whole body is arched off the table and I'm screaming with pleasure.

When I'm limp, he stands up, bends over and kisses me.

His cock is wet and hot against my belly. I push him off me and stand up. I take him in both of my hands and stroke him. Without letting go, I kneel and glide my mouth down on him.

He grunts, wraps his hand round my neck.

"That's it Temptress, just like that."

I drop one hand to his balls, play with them, and smile when he grunts again. I love hearing those growly sounds.

Just when I think he's getting closer to orgasm, he pulls back. I moan.

"Next time. I want to come inside you."

"That's what you said last time. I want you to come in my mouth like I did."

Indecision flickers across his face.

I wrap my hand round him and take him into my mouth again. Each time I suck up and down his cock, my hand follows.

Soon, Julian's thrusting against my mouth, groaning hoarsely, and my heart soars when he loses control and shouts my name, his cum spurting down my throat.

He carries me to the couch, and we lie down with my back against his front. I must have fallen asleep because when I wake up, Julian's stroking my breasts. He plays with my nipples until they are as hard as pebbles. Arrows of pleasure shoot through my body.

I reach my hand back around his neck as he nibbles on mine. He caresses the side of my hip and angles my butt. When he penetrates me, the burn is a heady mixture of pleasure and pain.

"You're so fucking tight, Temptress."

"I love your nickname for me."

He chokes on a laugh when I move back against him.

"You okay?" He asks.

"Will you move already? I've waited over three years for this."

He laughs again.

Then he adjusts us so that one of his arms stretches out alongside mine. He intertwines our hands.

He drives into me, lazily at first, then faster, his free hand holding me in place for him.

"I love you, Winona Smith." He punctuates each word with a powerful thrust.

My body is a mass of bliss. I just make out his words.

"Who's your man, Temptress?"

I push back against him. I'm so close to orgasm; it's all I can think about.

"Say it! Who's your man?"

"Julian! You're my man!"

He rubs my clit, and I explode, bucking against him.

Julian screams against my neck and holds me tightly as his hot cum shoots up my channel.

"I love you too," I say when I can speak.

Epilogue
Julian

Three Months later

IT'S MY WEDDING DAY. I've never been as nervous as I am today. I'm convinced Winona will not turn up. The feeling is killing me.

I wait for her at the altar. The whole town seems to be packed inside the church. Everyone is chattering happily, therefore I try to smile. I know it doesn't happen when my lips refuse to cooperate.

The wedding march starts. People return to their seats. Everyone hushes.

I watch the back of the church. The flower girls and ring boys come out first. They are all my temptress' nephews and nieces. I've been on my own most of my life, but the last two months, Winona's family became mine too. I've become an uncle, cousin, son and grandson.

Winona's bridesmaids, friends from school and college, follow. Then comes Ella, my temptress' best friend who's the maid of honor.

Finally, Winona comes into sight, accompanied by her father, and I breathe a sigh of relief.

She sees me. My heart settles.

Her eyes remain on my face as she strolls up the aisle, even when her father hands her to me, as if she knows how anxious I've been.

Throughout the ceremony, I can't stop feeling grateful. I never thought I'd find someone who gets me the way Winona does. I know I can be overpowering and demanding. There are times I want her all to myself. She understands.

It doesn't mean she takes all my craziness. She pushes back when she believes I'm crossing over a line she's not comfortable with. That's part of the reason I love her. Because with her, I can be me without worrying I'll hurt or upset her. She's strong enough not to take any shit from me.

"Do you take this woman to be your lawfully wedded wife, forsaking all others, for as long as you both shall live?" The pastor asks.

"I do," I say, looking into Winona's champagne eyes.

When she affirms she takes me as her lawfully wedded husband, her voice is just as sure as mine.

We exchange the rings we commissioned together. I put a lot of thought into the designs of these rings because they are a visual symbol that she's mine. Whenever she looks at the ring on her finger, I want Winona to think of the care I put into its design and know how much I love her. Know I'm the only man she's allowed to think about, just like she's the only woman on my mind.

"I pronounce you man and wife."

I take her into my arms and kiss her forehead. Then I kiss her mouth like a thirsty man, because for the last seven days, her family wouldn't allow us to be together. It was a tradition I wasn't very fond of.

Our guests go crazy, clapping, laughing and even whistling. The pastor clears his throat. Reluctantly, I tear my mouth away.

"Later, Lothario," Winona whispers against my ear.

"Yes, Temptress," I whisper back.

I can't wait to start my life with her.

MARRYING THE BIG MOUNTAIN MAN

CURVY BRIDES OF BLOSSOM FORD BOOK 7

IRIS WEST

Chapter 1
Keisha

AS THE MOUNTAINS of Blossom Ford, Arizona, come into view, my heart settles down a little. They look as breathtaking as they did in the photos Barret, my matched groom, sent. I might be taking the greatest risk of my life, but at least I'll be doing it in a place that sings to my soul.

I signed up to Blossom Ford Matchmaking Agency's Mail-Order bride program on a whim, still, deciding to marry Barrett came from a place inside that connected with the type of person he is. My lips tilt up as I remember the words he used to introduce himself:

"I'm a big, callous ridden, rough around the edges man. Your life won't be easy, but you'll have the satisfaction of knowing you've worked hard for your keep and the solace of being among nature's beauty. I can't give you sweet words, however you can expect a committed and hard-working man who'll provide for our family."

The words and their tone told me so much about my prospective husband.

He's offering what I'm searching for. A lasting marriage based on mutual trust, understanding and a will to make it work.

I've experienced first-hand the hurt and betrayal a passionate relationship brings and have decided to have nothing to do with it.

Mom and Dad were so happy in the early years of my life, I thought I was the luckiest girl alive. By the time I got to middle school, I stayed out as much as possible to avoid their arguing. They are the best of friends now, but before they divorced, my lovely parents had turned into two warring enemies.

Despite being jaded, I tried dating. I figured what I'd learned from seeing my parents fight and my desire and determination to have a healthy relationship gave me an advantage. It took forever to find a boyfriend. It turns out not many guys want to date a girl who's taller and bigger than them.

Eventually, I found someone who I thought might be the man of my dreams. It didn't last long.

"Baby, expecting me to sleep only with you is unreasonable. I thought you understood I'm a free guy. And I like variety," he'd said when I caught him cheating with a girl at least three times skinnier than me.

I hadn't understood. After that, I just couldn't bring myself to believe in passionate love. The pain of being in love didn't seem worth it to me.

Someone at work mentioned modern mail-order brides, horrified at the idea of a loveless marriage. The more I thought about it, the more sense it made sense. After I turned twenty-five and was made redundant for the second time in my life, I looked into it and came across Barrett's profile.

The train slows as it eases into Blossom Ford. I get up and gather my rucksack and suitcase. I'm about to open the door when it's wrenched back. A word of thanks is on the tip of my tongue when a huge hand reaches out and effortlessly lifts my suitcase down before I can reach it.

"Thank you," I say after I exit the train. I gaze up and up. It's an unusual thing for me. Being nearly six feet, I'm the person who usually looks down. He must be at least six feet and six inches tall. A thrill runs through me. I'm such a sucker for tall men.

"Hi Keisha. I'm Barret."

His profile picture doesn't do him justice.

He's not a pretty man, yet I've met no one hotter. Thick, arched eyebrows frame his hazel eyes. A brown beard flanks lips meant to bring pleasure to a woman. Shoulder-length chestnut hair with blonde highlights reaches the top of his shoulders.

Heat flushes my cheeks. I realize I've ignored his outstretched hand while ogling him and flush again. I've always thought of my hands as huge, but my hand feels tiny in his much larger one.

All the chit-chat I prepared vanishes from my mind. Butterflies fill my tummy.

"It's nice to meet you," my voice is annoyingly croaky.

"You too. Let me take your rucksack."

"It's alright, I can carry it."

"You look like you can, but you've been traveling for hours. It's no trouble to me." He stretches his hand out like he won't accept no for an answer.

I'm so used to taking care of my own things, I'm ruffled for a moment. But then I remind myself I decided to embrace this new life.

I pass him the heavy bag and watch as he lugs it onto his back like it weighs nothing.

A whistle rings.

"Come on, the train is about to depart."

I follow Barrett down the platform, startled to notice I am the only person to get off the train.

There's a small parking lot outside with two trucks. Barrett leads me to the oldest one and as he stows my luggage in the trunk, I glance toward the sprawling town. Just breathing the air makes me feel good. I close my eyes and stare up at the sky, luxuriating in the hot rays of the sun.

"Great, isn't it?"

My eyes fly open. Barrett is facing the mountains, admiration and pride emanating from his easy stance.

"I can feel the difference in air quality between here and Garnet City."

He goes to the passenger side and opens the door.

Something warm moves in my chest.

It's not just because I can't remember if any man has ever done that for me, it's the casual way he opens the door, like that's how he was brought up. It's so unlike his description of himself.

I get in the truck and watch as Barret closes the door and stalks around to the driver's seat. His height, burly chest and long legs as thick as tree trunks don't stop him from moving gracefully.

"Do you want to grab a quick bite before we head to the registry office?"

"I had a snack on the train."

I washed my face and freshened my makeup, too. Even though I am a cleanser and cream only girl, I plan on getting married only once; I want to look my best.

My ivory dress reaches just above my knees and shows my curves to what I hope is perfection. I had my hair pressed at the hairdresser yesterday and took great care to make sure it doesn't frizz. I swapped my heels for sneakers during my journey, but changed again when I freshened up.

"I was expecting more luggage," Barrett says as he drives away from the train station.

"Disappointed?"

"Hell no! If anything, I'm in awe."

"Clothes shopping is not a favorite. I keep a couple of nice dresses, but the rest of my clothes are jeans."

"I'm the same, so I'm glad to hear that."

"You have a couple of dresses too?"

Barrett chuckles. The sound is big and booming like him.

My heart skips a beat at the way his face transforms. He looks younger, more approachable.

As we drive through town, Barret points out places I might need to visit. He stops the truck after only a ten-minute ride outside an imposing building.

"We're here." He switches off the engine of the powerful car and faces me. "It's not too late to change your mind."

There's a steadiness in his voice that calms me. I'm surer now than when I left the city I grew up in.

"I'm sure."

I return his gaze, wanting him to see how determined I am.

When I responded to his request, he'd written back, saying I was too young to settle into the hard life of the mountain and he was too old for me. It took a lot to convince him my twenty-five years of age didn't diminish my desire for the type of life he was offering and that his age was a plus for me. I enjoyed living in the city, but I wouldn't miss it. I wanted a mature man who was ready to settle down, not a younger man not ready to be exclusive.

He nods and I sigh.

After he climbs out of the truck, I check my make-up one more time, reminding myself Barrett Montgomery is the man I decided to marry with a contract in order to build a strong marriage and a family. Passion doesn't come into it. Attraction is fine, it'll help things in the bedroom. However, falling in love is forbidden.

The success of this marriage is important to me. If I'm the only one who falls in love and Barret finds out, it might invalidate our contract. And that's something I don't want. So I tell my heart to stop being moved by his gentlemanly behavior and kindness.

Chapter 2

Barrett

I'M DOING THE RIGHT thing, I tell myself as I stand beside Keisha in one of the registry office rooms, waiting for the officiant to start the wedding ceremony. This is the best way to ensure what happened to Dad doesn't happen to me.

I thought I was over my childish desire for a large family of my own, however the last few years I've longed for companionship, someone to share my evenings with. I resisted the urge for so long, but I guess what my grandaddy and the townsfolk used to say about Montgomery men not being able to live on their own is true after all.

Grandaddy also used to say Montgomery men fall head over heels with one woman only and love only her despite how cruel she might be. Dad loved Mom until his last day, even though she abandoned him a year after their marriage, when I was only three months old.

I'm making sure I don't lose my head over some woman who isn't suited for mountain living. I'm getting hitched on my own terms. With a partner who has the same values as I do and wants a lasting, solid marriage based on family.

It's just I didn't expect to be nervous. Maybe everyone gets nervous on their wedding day, whether or not they are in love.

Keisha certainly does. She's clasping the small bouquet in her hands as if it can hold her up. Yet she's standing straight, the determined look in her chocolate brown eyes and the tilt of her firm chin making me feel better.

She's the most beautiful woman I've ever seen. I wasn't expecting a wedding gown. She's stunning in a simple ivory dress that reaches her elbows and knees. I'm used to towering over women, but the top of her silky head reaches my shoulders. It's the perfect height to pull her in close, kiss her bow shaped bottom lip and caress her delectable curves.

I'm grateful when Mr. Rose, the officiant, starts the ceremony and pulls my mind from the direction it's taking. I focus on the words he's saying. I'm only marrying once, and I intend to follow my vows.

"Barrett, do you take this woman to be your wife, to live together in matrimony, to love, honor and comfort her, in sickness and in health, forsaking all others, for as long as you both shall live?"

"Yes," I answer, my eyes on Keisha. The possessive tone of my voice surprises me, but I don't hide it. It's best she sees me for who I am.

Her gaze is steady on me as she accepts to take me as her husband.

She's mine the moment she says yes.

We exchange the gold rings I bought and the simple ceremony we both chose is over.

"You may kiss the bride."

I take Keisha's hands in mine, holding the flowers with her. The band on her ring finger glides against my rough palm. Her eyes widen.

I lean in, looking at her, and stop a breath from her mouth. She closes the distance between us.

Satisfaction and something else rise in me. I want to growl. The desire to taste her is so strong, I have to hold myself back, lest I scare her away.

I press my lips against hers. Softness and sweetness push back. It's the most innocent of touches yet, when I reluctantly pull back, it leaves me wanting more.

Mr. Rose insists on taking a couple of pictures in the sunny garden outside. He's not satisfied until Keisha and I have our arms around each other and are smiling at the camera.

"It was kind of the officiant to take a photo of us," Keisha says as we enter the car.

My lips tug up. "You mean interfering, right?"

"He was pushy, like a grandfather or an uncle. Is he a family member?"

"He and Dad were school friends. Now Dad is not around anymore. Now and then, he feels like it's his place to make sure I'm doing the right thing."

Mr. Rose had always been like that, especially during the time I was younger.

"That's nice."

Is that longing in Keisha's voice?

"You might not think that when you can't go more than a few yards without someone asking how you are doing because they haven't seen you for a while. Most of the time, it's nosiness."

"I still think I'd prefer that to people not noticing my absence."

"Let's see how you feel in ten, twenty years."

Keisha looks at the bouquet in her hands. Her hair hides her face.

I fight the desire to pull that curtain of silk behind her ear and turn her toward me.

When she finally gazes at me, there's a smile around her lips and eyes.

"Let's do that."

"Do you want to go to a restaurant?"

Keisha bites her lip. "I can last a couple of hours if that's what you'd like to do, but I'd prefer to shower and wear something comfortable. These shoes are killing me."

I'm smiling from ear to ear. It was definitely the right decision to pick my life partner based on compatibility.

"Take them off."

Keisha bites her bottom lip again, two white teeth worrying the nude, perfect bow.

A bolt of desire shoots straight for my cock.

About to strip my suit jacket and tie, I change my mind and remove only the tie. I toss it to the back of the truck and leave my suit jacket to serve as cover for my groin.

Keisha slips her feet out of her ivory shoes and sighs.

"That bad?"

"It's hard to find shoes that fit. Even if they're the right size, they're uncomfortable soon after wearing them. I suppose trainers are okay for you. Do you have trouble getting formal shoes?"

"I only have a couple of pairs. I had them specially made."

Even sneakers were hard to find in my size. It used to bother me when I was in middle and high school. Not anymore. A few pairs of boots are all I need, anyway.

As I drive off toward the mountain, with Keisha sitting beside me, a feeling I can't place settles within me. I put it down to a sense of belonging with another person. I came down the mountain single. Now, I have a family, someone I'm responsible for.

I'm sure that's also what's got me wanting to whistle and is making the greenery on the mountain especially beautiful today.

"How long does it take to get to the top of the mountains? Have you tried it?"

"It depends on whether you go up the beaten track or take the routes only locals know. It can take the best part of a day or a few hours."

When I was younger, I used to go every time I fought with Dad. Sometimes, my best friend Verlin O'Connor and I would roam the mountains for fun.

"What happens if you're halfway up and it's nighttime? I'd be terrified in the woods at night."

"These woods are safer than many places. Most people go up on organized tours."

Keisha's gaze wanders, taking in everything around her.

My wife.

She wants the same things I do. Which is how I want it always to be. That's why that unfamiliar feeling in my chest can only be a sense of responsibility, belonging, and possession.

Whenever Dad got drunk, he'd talk about Mom, reminiscing over the early days of their marriage when Mom was still infatuated with the mountain. It was painful to watch. Mom's name was the last thing he said before he passed.

He never got over her. As a kid, I blamed him for not leaving with Mom. Now, I understand why he couldn't. These woods are part of me.

I'm already in lust with Keisha. Her intoxicating scent of mint, the warm tone of her mocha skin that seems to invite my touch, and her curvaceous body is playing havoc with my self-control.

I want my wife. There's nothing wrong with that.

I already like her inquisitive nature and respect her determination to make this marriage work, just like me, and that's fine, too. The only thing that would be wrong is falling head over heels for her. However, that will not happen, because my whole being knows better than to allow myself to go through what Dad did.

Chapter 3
Keisha

WE PULL THROUGH a gate with the sign Montgomery Chicken Farm into a huge yard. Barrett stops in front of a large wooden cabin. I recognize it from the photos he sent.

I unbuckle my seat belt and slip my shoes back on. Barrett swings my door open and I step down from the truck, bag on my shoulder.

"This is our home," he sounds gruff, yet I hear pride in his booming voice. Warmth spreads through me when I process the word our.

Without warning, he picks me up. One moment I'm standing awkwardly in front of him and the next I'm being swept up into his arms, like a dainty damsel in distress.

Surprise has my arms locking around his neck. A laugh escapes me.

Barret stalks toward the front door. Before I can fumble to open it, he shoves the door back with one foot.

"Welcome home, Mrs. Montgomery!"

I can't look away from him. I'm held in his hazel eyes, trapped by the promise of heat I see there. My heart beats faster. A bleat breaks the near silence in the yard.

"That's Angelina, the kindest of our goats. I guess she's welcoming you."

The spell is broken. Barrett puts me down.

As soon as his hands fall off my waist, I'm wanting them back there. Feeling hot and a little dazed, I wander around the living room of the wooden cabin. I need space away from Barrett.

There's a comfortable old sofa along one wall and an imposing, antique chest opposite it. A picture of a young-looking Barrett and a man sits proudly on it. There's another picture, but this was clearly taken at a family photo studio.

"Is this you?" I point to the baby in the studio photo.

He nods. "That's Dad and my mother."

"You were cute."

Barrett raises a bushy eyebrow. "That's past tense. Am I no longer cute?"

Is he kidding me? He's so cute right now, with his hands tucked into his trouser pockets and the ghost of a smile playing around his lips. I want to sidle up to him and kiss that raised eyebrow. Instead, I shrug.

"Your Mom is pretty. Do your parents live nearby?"

He removes his hands from his pant pockets.

"Dad passed a few years ago. Mom doesn't live around here." He walks toward the front door. "I'll grab your stuff."

I stare at his back as he marches outside.

AS I FINISH dressing, the sun is setting. I listen out for Barret, wondering if he is back from checking on the animals. One more glance in the mirror convinces me I've done everything possible to look good in a pair of my most comfortable yet sexy jeans and a V-neck top that shows my cleavage to its best.

I glance at the massive bed, my side of the closet, and my toiletries on the dresser. He must have more stuff than me, even so Barret left more than half of the space everywhere for me. I wanted a new start, so only brought what I thought would be useful here and sold the rest. My paltry belongings hardly cover the space he created for me.

The sheets on the bed and the curtains are old, but they are clean and pretty. It's comforting, knowing the furnishings in the cabin have been used by Barrett's ancestors, who are now my family.

The thought of sleeping with Barrett has me glancing at the bed again. Heat creeps up my cheeks when my core clenches. Alarmed, I accidentally slam the door as I rush out of the room.

"Are you okay?" Barrett asks as he enters the house.

I go hot all over.

"What are we having for dinner?" I ask and head to the kitchen, keeping myself as far apart from him as the house will allow.

I open the fridge, and for the first few seconds take in cold air, while pretending to scope it out.

I feel Barret come up behind me. His hands touch the sides of my shoulders.

I want to lean back and have his arms wrap around me. We're married after all. That would be perfectly normal.

"I'll cook today. Sit and rest."

I blink. Barret steers me toward the kitchen table.

I sink into a chair and pretend to watch the orange and pink glow of the setting sun through the kitchen window.

Barret gets ingredients, chops them, and starts cooking something. Once I feel safe he's concentrating on his task, my eyes wander back to him, tracking his every movement.

For such a big man, he's agile and graceful when he moves, which is so unlike clumsy me. He cooks like someone who's been doing something for a long time and can do it with their eyes closed. His butt looks good in the jeans he changed into and his back and arm muscles ripple as he reaches for utensils.

"Like what you see?"

"What do you mean?" I play with the crochet patterns on the tablecloth. "This is pretty. Who made it?"

"My granny. She used patterns from tablecloths my great grannies used but were too old to carry on using." He places a salad on the table.

"Really? It must bring you such a sense of belonging. I love that."

"Change whatever you want, to make the place into something you like."

If he keeps being this generous, it won't be long before I'm completely in love with him. "The dress I wore today was my mom's wedding dress. She's much slimmer than me, so the seamstress used the cloth below the knees to enlarge the sides to fit me. I love knowing others, especially people I love have used whatever I'm wearing."

"You were sexy in it. I bet the thoughts going through your mind when you were eying me a little while ago don't come close to the ones I had when I saw you in that gorgeous dress." Barret says. Then he turns and heads for the cooker.

I'm so glad he's not looking at me right now. I'm as pleased as a schoolgirl being told by her prom date that she's stunning.

He finds me attractive. At the very least, he thinks I was attractive in my wedding dress.

That makes me bold. I watch him until he brings two steaming plates of stew to the table. We eat mostly in silence. At first, I'm a little worried Barrett is bored and am tempted to make casual conversation, but I decide to behave the way I usually do. That's what we agreed on. To be ourselves, to not try to be something other than what we are.

Then, I realize the silence is comfortable. We both have more stew. When I finish that, I sip wine as he polishes off another plate.

I insist on washing up, still, Barrett decides to help by rinsing.

"They'll air dry," he says as I grab a dishcloth.

"Can we sit outside for a bit?"

Barrett grabs the bottle of wine, a beer, and a blanket. I take my wine glass and follow him out and around the porch to the back of the cabin until we reach a porch seat.

My mouth opens as I spy the view ahead. A mountain slope and trees rise toward the dark sky. The soft noise of babbling reaches my ears, but I can't see any water.

"Is there a stream nearby?"

He points to his left. I don't see it at first. When I do, I'm awed again. I've seen nothing more picturesque.

"You must sit here every day. I've been staring for only what must be a few minutes and I feel the tranquility of the mountain."

"Most days. It's not always tranquil though."

We sit and appreciate the view.

"Some visitors to the lodge further up the mountain can be loud."

"Is that the generator? I know you explained about electricity and internet out here but I'm still surprised you have decent Wi-Fi." I point to a large device.

Barrett made sure I knew about the difficulties I might face living out here.

"We use it if there's a power cut. With an external antenna installed, Wi-Fi is not too bad."

Barrett spreads the blanket over my knees. "Even though it's summer, up here, it gets a little chilly at night."

We sit down and peer at the mountain. I can feel Barrett sitting close to me and hear the lulling sound of the stream. I'm both comforted and on edge, my body alive and full of anticipation.

Chapter 4

Barrett

I REMOVE THE WINEGLASS from Keisha's limp hand and place it on the floor. She's just as striking with her eyes closed as she's awake.

She's leaning back against the bench and snoring lightly. Unbidden, my hand reaches toward her face. I stop it before it can trace her lips and touch her face.

I shake my head. It's been too long since I got laid. I must be needing the warmth the body of a woman can provide. And Keisha is my type of woman.

Carefully, I lift her. This close, it's not just her mint scent I can smell. Something else stirs my nose. A fragrance that must be all Keisha, feminine and earthy.

Carrying a woman shouldn't be this good. Keisha feels right in my arms, as if she's meant to be held by me alone. She doesn't wake as I enter the house, the bedroom, and sit down so I can pull back the sheets on her side of the bed.

Even when I stand up and walk round to place her on the bed, she sleeps like a baby. I lay her down and cover her before I head out of the room, collect the glasses from the porch and shut the cabin down for the night.

In the bedroom, I strip off my shirt in the soft light of the moon, but the moment my hands reach for the zipper on my jeans, I pause. I don't want Keisha to be startled if she wakes and finds herself sleeping with a naked man. Even if that man is her husband. I can sleep in my jeans for one night.

I slip into bed, fold my hands and tuck them under my head. So much for my well-laid plan. I look at Keisha again, but she's still sleeping soundly. I'll just have to start it tomorrow.

She's lying so close to me it's fucking hard not to reach out and touch her. I really don't know how I'll cope tomorrow night when I execute my plan for day one and hold her in my arms.

THE SUN IS shining brightly and soaking the cabin and farm in its hot rays. Keisha comes out of the house and stands on the porch, her face turned upward. I stop throwing chicken feed and watch as she stretches, tits straining against her blouse.

She spots me and drops her arms. She's a little shy and I'm perverted enough to like it. I watch her walk toward me, hips swaying tantalizingly.

"I'm sorry I fell asleep on our wedding night."

She's worrying that gorgeous bottom lip again. I feast my eyes for another beat.

"We have today."

"Right." She looks at the chickens as if she's never seen hens before. "What can I do? I saw the note you left about starting the chores and made breakfast."

"Let's eat."

Inside the house, I wash up while Keisha dishes bacon, eggs and sausages.

"I'll go out with you and learn the chores," Keisha says once I'm back in the kitchen.

I nod and tuck into the food she made. "How do you feel? Did you sleep well?"

She gives me a sideways glance, then focuses on her food. "I've already apologized for falling asleep."

A chuckle erupts out of me. She's so easy to tease. "Keisha, you had a hard, long day. It isn't every day a woman gets married, especially a marriage like ours. Even if it's something you wanted to do, I'm sure you had a few worries. It couldn't have been easy trusting a man you've never met. I really want to know if you were okay sleeping in a strange bed."

"I guess I'm a little embarrassed." She tucks hairs that escaped her ponytail behind her ears. "Usually, I have a hard time falling asleep in unfamiliar places. I must have been more exhausted than I thought I was because the last thing I remembered when I got up was taking in that scenic view last night."

We finish our meal and while she's doing dishes; I get a gift-wrapped box from the bedroom.

"What is it?" She asks as I hand it to her.

"Put them on. They aren't pretty, but will keep your feet safer than your sneakers."

As she opens the box and puts on the boots I gifted her, I grab jugs and a pair of gloves.

"Thank you! They feel comfortable."

Warmth spreads all over me.

"I got your shoe size from the information the matchmaking agency sent."

Needing cool air, I head outside. When Keisha joins me, I give her a tour of the farm and explain the different chores that need doing. Her dark brown eyes are enormous and she stops me to ask questions.

I collected eggs earlier, but there are a few more in the nesting boxes, so I take those out.

"I didn't realize how big the farm is. There are so many chickens. What do you do with the eggs?"

"The bakery in town takes half of them, and the rest go to the restaurants and local shops."

Her eyes widen even more when we reach the vegetable garden and I remember she mentioned a love of gardening.

"Can we harvest some vegetables?"

She's so excited, I can't help laughing. "This afternoon. I guess this can be one of your chores."

I shepherd her toward the goats. "These beauties are going to be cranky if I don't milk them now."

"This is Angelina." I march the goat toward the stand and milk her.

"How do you know?" Keisha peers at the goat.

"See this black dot on her nose?"

Keisha nods.

"Seraphina and Isabella don't have it."

"Let me try," Keisha says after she's watched me milk Seraphina.

She grabs Isabella, the youngest goat, and shepherds her out of the goat pen like I did.

"She's following me!"

I help her put the goat in the stand when the latch doesn't close properly.

"It isn't coming out," she says after a few pulls on Isabella's udder.

I place my hands on hers and guide the movement of her fingers.

"It's working!"

There are small flecks of gold in Keisha's eyes.

That unfamiliar feeling is back. Whatever the hell it is, has my heart pounding. I can't tear my eyes away from Keisha's innocent, delighted face.

"Let me try by myself," she says, and the spell is broken.

I blink and slip my fingers away.

She's focused on what she's doing and looks as excited as a kid who's learned to ride a bike for the first time. The milk is coming in spurts, but I can tell that with a little more practice, she'll do a great job.

We have lunch and spend the afternoon doing more chores. She's eager to help but, by the time we seat to eat the stew I warmed up for us, I can tell she's going to be sore tomorrow.

"When did you make all this delicious food?" She fails to hide a yawn.

"My cooking is not nearly as delicious as this. Mr. Jackson, a friend of Dad's, gave it to me a couple of days ago. I'll introduce you when we go into town."

"From Jackson's Diner?"

How did she know?

Keisha laughs. "Did you know you raise your left eyebrow if something surprises you?"

"It's a habit I can't seem to shake."

"Jackson's Diner is one of the most visited places in Blossom Ford, Arizona," she announces. "I wanted to find out a bit more about the place I'd be living in and did some research."

"You worked hard today!"

"Do I get a reward?"

Hot damn! She may be thinking of an innocent reward, yet my mind conjures a different picture.

I must have given something away because the amusement in her eyes is replaced by awareness.

"Later. In a few days." I meant to whisper it, but a growl emerges instead.

Keisha bites her bottom lip, then tucks into her food.

She lasts an hour outside before she admits she has to turn in. I do a round of the farm while she readies for bed. By the time I enter the bedroom, she's lying down.

I smile when she blinks up at the ceiling. She's trying so hard to stay awake. I strip, place my clothes on the rocking chair in the room's corner and pad to the bed. Keisha is staring at my cock. It stirs, as if inviting her gaze, and I realize how much I enjoy her watching me. I get into bed and look at her.

"Come here. Let me hug you."

She slides closer and lays her head on my chest. I wrap my arms around her and pull her slightly up my body.

"Comfortable?"

"Yes."

I frown at how low her voice is. She wrote no to the virgin question on the agency's questionnaire.

"I sleep with my birthday costume on. Does it make you uncomfortable?"

She shakes her head.

I rub one hand up and down the silky material covering her back. It's so good to have her pressed against the side of my body.

"For the next few days, I'm just going to hug you like this. It'll give us some time to get to know each other. Tell me if you feel uncomfortable."

"I like this," Keisha's voice is stronger this time.

"So do I."

It's the sweetest torture I've ever felt. She must be wearing shorts because I can feel the soft skin of her legs as they lay beside mine. I breathe in and out steadily and try not to think about the softness of her tits, squashed against my side.

"Goodnight sweetheart." I kiss her forehead.

She's tense for a moment, then relaxes.

"Goodnight Barrett!

Three days. My plan is to give her three days to settle down on the farm and get used to being together before we have sex. This is only the first night and I'm already fucked. I want to rip her clothes and eat her up until she's screaming with pleasure.

Chapter 5
Keisha

I'VE BEEN AT THE farm for four days and have already fallen in love with the vegetable garden, the animals and the mountain. This morning I only felt a few twinges in my body, so even the soreness I had after helping with the chores the first couple of days has subsided. The only problem? I'm falling in love with the farm owner.

We've settled into a nice routine. Barrett wakes up at the crack of dawn and starts working. I make breakfast about an hour later and we eat together before I help on the farm. I return to the cabin to make lunch and sometimes we have that outside.

I help a little more in the afternoons before showering and cooking dinner.

It's late afternoon now. My hair is tied up in a towel and I'm finishing dinner when Barrett walks in the door. He glances at my bare legs. I swear I can see heat in his eyes before he turns and heads to the bathroom.

I don't know what's going through his mind. He looks at me like a man starved of sex one minute, the next he's like the Santas Mom and Dad used to take me to when I was little; all sweet, kind, and cuddly.

I lay the table and dish up. By the time I'm finished, Barrett is in the kitchen, the combination of his wet hair and beard, citrus shower gel scent and low-slung pants making my mouth water.

After dinner, Barrett grabs my glass of wine and a beer for him.

"I have to do my hair. I'll stay here."

Barrett freezes. "Why?"

"It goes everywhere. And I have to moisturize it. You might not like that."

"I won't know until I see it," he says after studying me for what feels like ages.

I shrug, grab my comb, moisturizer, and a couple of scrunchies and head outside. His beer and my glass of wine are on the floor beside the seat. He has a can of beer every night. I guess the hard work of the farm takes care of the calories he ingests.

I can only hope that the physical labor I'm doing will offset the daily glass of wine I've been drinking.

I unwrap the towel and rub it around my head. My hair takes forever to dry. Barrett is staring at it. I can't tell if he's shocked. My long, silky, pressed hair is gone. In its place is a mass of tight curls.

I warned him.

Using the comb, I part a small section, pat dry the ends and carefully comb through it to detangle the hair.

"Can I do that?"

I gawk at him.

"It's got to be easier if I do it, right?"

I hold out the towel and comb.

When he takes it, I sit cross-legged on the floor.

He takes my spot on the bench. I feel his hands on my head and ready myself for the sting of pulled hair.

"You're gentler than my mom," I say after he's done nearly half of my head. His hands are massive, I didn't expect him to be so gentle.

"Did she do your hair like this?"

"When I was very little. One day she wasn't well. Dad had to do it. His braids weren't as pretty as Mom's, but his hands were gentler. From then on, I threw a tantrum if Mom tried to do it."

"I can't imagine that."

Now I know his voice well enough, to make out he's amused.

"I was very bratty before Mom and Dad divorced."

Barrett is quiet for a moment. "I'm guessing it wasn't amicable."

Now it's my turn to be amused by the caution in his voice. This is why I'm falling for him. There's a gentleness in him I didn't really expect. He's perceptive, too.

"It was hell. I was twelve and couldn't understand why our happy world was collapsing." I hug my knees and stare at the wilderness of the mountain. "But now they are the best of friends. Mom met and married a Spanish man shortly after. It took Dad a couple of years to date again. He's married and has two kids. It wasn't until they were both happy that I realized their new partners suit them better."

"Who did you live with?"

"Dad. Until I finished high school and started working. Then he and my stepmom moved up North to be closer to her family."

"It's done," Barrett says.

He hands me the comb and shifts back to his place.

I moisturize and quickly make two French braids, conscious of Barrett watching my hands as he drinks chilled beer.

"Are you trying to learn to braid?"

"Yes. We may have a girl. She might prefer my hands."

I'm in love with this man.

There's no more avoiding it. I've fallen for the way he holds me and makes me feel safe. The way he looks out and cares for me. At that moment, I'm sure if we have kids, he'll do everything to protect and keep them safe.

If only he's as eager as me to start making babies, everything would be perfect.

"What was that?"

Heat races all over my body. Did I say that aloud?

"Nothing." I stand. "I'm going to turn in."

I can't make out the expression in Barrett's eyes.

I gather my things and go into the house. I wear a camisole and short set I got especially for after the wedding and get into bed, thinking about when Barrett is planning on having a child. Perhaps I need to be more proactive and start things?

The door swings open. I watch Barrett as he strips and pads toward me. My womb clenches, my nipples harden. His size doesn't surprise me anymore, but I can't help wondering again if he'll fit inside me. The fact that he's aware of my scrutiny turns me on even more. I love cuddling up to his hard, hot body, but it's no longer enough.

How does a wife ask her husband for sex?

"Do you want to sleep?" Barrett says as he gets into bed.

"No!"

He leans over me and caresses my bottom lip with the tip of one finger.

I suck my breath.

His finger presses along the seam of my lips. When I open my mouth a little, he slides his finger in. I pull on it. Darts of pleasure shoot to my core.

"Keisha, I want to fuck the hell out of you!"

Barrett's growl makes me wet. I have no problem making out the expression in his eyes now. I wrap my arms around his neck and pull him down.

He kisses me hard, his tongue dueling against mine. It's just what I'm craving.

His enormous hands tug at the bottom of my top and slide it up my chest. I lift and let him take it off me.

"Ah sweetheart." He stares at my breasts then palms them.

"These fit in my hands." He squeezes them so they push together, his big thumbs caressing my pebbled nipples.

I moan.

He plays with my nipples, first licking, then suckling them until I think I'm going to orgasm.

"Barrett." It's a hoarse whisper.

"What?"

He blows on my breasts, the cool air making my puckered nipples harder. My hips lift of their own accord.

"Barrett?"

"Tell me."

He slides down my body, grabs my shorts and panties, and rips them.

"You're so pretty, Keisha. I'm going to love eating this pussy."

My hips lift again. My tongue moistens my dry lips.

"Say it Sweetheart. What do you want?"

"Touch me there."

I don't care anymore how embarrassing asking him to touch and kiss my private parts is. I need relief now.

"That's it, Sweetheart."

Barrett's hand snakes past my bare mound and flicks the top of my clit. He strokes the opening of my pussy.

"I love how wet you are."

With his slippery fingers, he rubs my clit, their roughness and his speed providing the right pressure. I grip the sheets as tension mounts in my core and reaches an unbearable point. My pussy contracts, tipping me over the edge, and I explode.

Barrett tongues my juices and aftershocks quake through me.

He slides up my body, kisses my breasts, then the side of my neck.

"That was part of your reward," his whisper is rough against my ear.

I barely have time to work out what he means before I feel his cock pushing against my slippery entrance.

I slide my hand between our bodies and stroke up and down his thick cock before guiding him into me.

He hisses and bites my neck.

Moisture seeps out of me.

Then he's stretching me. I inhale and he pauses, breathing hard. He growls words that flush my entire body and turn me on.

Soon, I'm ready for more of him and lift my hips. His big cock surges a little further into me again and again until it's buried to the hilt.

Initially, Barrett sets a languid pace. His hands rove over my body and he bites my earlobes till I'm undulating against him.

Then he grabs my butt and fucks me hard, his hard, long pennis driving in and out of me until I'm keening his name.

He rubs my clit, and I contract around him, screaming in pleasure.

Barrett growls and spills hot seed into me. When he's still, he flips us so I'm lying on top of him, in the position we slept in since our wedding day.

As pleasure aftershocks ripple through my body and Barrett's big hand slides up and down my back, a question rises in my mind, even as my eyes flutter close.

Will I be able to keep my feelings hidden from my husband?

Chapter 6
Barrett

IT'S A WEEK SINCE Keisha and I slept together, and I can't remember a time I was happier. We work hard during the day, then fuck harder at night. She may not have had a lot of experience in the bedroom, but she meets every rough demand I make.

I pop my head out of a chicken coop and peer at the thick drops of rain pounding the yard. Even though I'm wearing a sturdy anorak and knee-high waterproof boots, the heavy rain found a way into my clothes.

The cabin door crashes open. Keisha stares out, then screams and dashes into the rain before I can holler at her to head back inside. I search for whatever alarmed her, my body coiled to spring into action.

Then I see the fox. I barrel down the yard toward Keisha, but it's too late.

She swings a broom toward the animal, yelling. It yelps and turns, then shrieks at Keisha, who swings the broom again.

My heart drops as Keisha loses her footing and falls. I miss her by a second.

"Are you okay?"

My heart is in my mouth as I look her over, checking she has hurt nothing.

"There's a fox." She tries to sit, but I stop her.

"It's gone."

"What about the chicken? Is it okay? The fox almost got it."

"For fuck's sake, Keisha! Will you lie still?"

She blinks up at me.

"Can you move your toes? And fingers?"

"Yes."

I carry her into the cabin and sit her down.

"I'm dropping mud on the chair. Let me clean up."

I stop her and crouch in front of her.

"Don't you ever do that again? Do you hear me?"

Keisha stares at me.

"Tell me you'll never put yourself in danger like that again. Not for anyone or anything?"

She nods.

I pull her down onto my lap and wrap my arms around her. Only when I feel the warmth of her soft body, does my heart slow down and I realize Keisha's patting my back.

"Barrett, we have to wash the mud off."

I take her into the shower, strip us down, and rinse the mud off. When we're both dry and dressed, I make her a hot chocolate.

"I'm going out for a bit," I say once she sips the sweet, dark brown liquid.

"In this rain?"

"I know these roads like the back of my hand. I'm used to driving in this weather, too."

"Let me get my anorak. I'll come with you."

I wrap a blanket around her.

"Stay warm."

Then I grab the truck key and flee the cabin. I drive down the mountain, slower than usual, because no matter what I told Keisha, it's dangerous to drive on the mountain roads while it's raining this hard.

Halfway down the mountain, I stop, slam out of the truck, and scream. I can't believe I've gone and fallen in love. I've done the very thing that made Dad's life a misery.

The worst thing is I've been lying to myself. I've been falling for her ever since I saw her through the window, when the train stopped outside Blossom Ford Station. I'm fascinated by her determination and courage, the way she works so damn hard even though she doesn't have to, and how she gives herself wholeheartedly to me.

Seeing her in danger only made me admit the truth.

I'm hopelessly in love with my wife.

I get back in the truck. Having to use all of my senses to prevent an accident stops me from thinking about Keisha, so I drive down the rest of the mountain.

Outside the O'Connor farm, I pull up. I desperately want the alcohol induced oblivion that I can find inside the bar, but I have to drive up the mountain. It's only four in the afternoon but no taxi will take me up there and I don't want to leave Keisha alone tonight. My friend Verlin is the only person who'd drive me up without a single question. It's a shame he's out of town.

A horn beeps behind me. It's old Jackson. He drives off and I follow him.

"What are you doing outside in this rain?" He asks when we are sitting in a booth in the diner after he's sent the waitress home.

The place is dead. It's no surprise, the way it's raining.

"Married life mistreating you already?"

Most people saw the grumpy and rough exterior of old man Jackson and mistakenly judged him as mean. But he's the kindest man I know. And he's sort of a second dad. Now and then, someone would say they saw Mom in some town and Dad would go searching for her. Until the age of eleven, I stayed with old man Jackson. After that, I took care of myself at home.

"Did Dad ever regret loving Mom?"

He narrows his eyes on me, bushy gray brows almost joining. "No."

My lip curls up.

"Some men will love two or three times, others love once. No matter how painful it is, it's a miracle to care for someone more than you do for yourself."

Is he talking about himself? As far as I know, only Dad, Verlin, and I know he's been in love with Mrs. Gallagher ever since she came to town as a young bride. Verlin and I overheard him talking with Dad.

Even though Mrs. Gallagher has been a widow for over thirty years, they are just friends. He won't say anything because he believes she's still in love with her dead husband.

"Some women are meant for the mountain, others are not, no matter how much they love their husbands. Have you talked to Keisha? I may be wrong, but I think she's the type that'll stay."

He's an excellent judge of character; I desperately want to believe him. I introduced Keisha to him a couple of days ago when we came down the mountain to deliver eggs.

I want to tell him to confess to Mrs. Gallagher, but I know better. He'll be mortified if I bring it up. It's better if he isn't aware Verlin and I know his secret.

"You better get back, it's getting dark. It'll be even harder to drive in this weather. Unless you want to kip down here tonight."

"Keisha's too new to the mountain. She'll be worried if I don't get back."

old man Jackson cracks up. The sound is gravelly. Whilst I was younger, I used to wonder if that was because he rarely laughed and so his laughing muscles were rusty.

"What's so funny?"

"You remind me of the old times with your dad. When we were younger."

"I'm leaving."

More laughter.

"Tell that O'Connor boy to stop sending me those bloody supplements. I'm not that old yet."

"Which one?"

"How the fuck should I know? There are so many of them."

Out of the nine O'Connor boys in Blossom Ford, Verlin is the only one who'd dare send supplements to old man Jackson. The old man knew that too.

I wave goodbye and sprint to the truck. It's a long drive back to the cabin. By the time I arrive, it's past dinnertime.

Keisha stands at the door, wrapped up in the blanket I gave her earlier.

God, I love her.

I don't know about tomorrow, but right now, I feel blessed I've had the chance to love her. Even as the realization crashes through me, a horrifying thought shoots its insidious claws into me.

What will I do if she ever wants to leave?

Chapter 7
Keisha

BARRETT HAS NOT BEEN the same since the day that damn fox snuck in our yard. That was four days ago. He's brooding over something but won't tell me what it is.

He's silent. Not Barrett silent, this is uncomfortable. I miss making love with him and having his arms around me as we go to sleep. I can see he still cares for me in the way he'll pick up a heavy load from me and carry it or when he slips a blanket over my shoulders while we sit outside.

However, he's staying outside longer. Yesterday, he went to the yard after dinner and didn't come in until I was in bed.

I bite my lip as he comes in. He takes me silently, then heads for the bathroom. I tell myself he's checking I'm okay, nevertheless the tension is getting to me.

Dinner is uncomfortable again.

"What's wrong? I've already said I'll be more careful, so what happened that day doesn't happen again. I don't know what to do to make things right."

I can't stand how awkward we've become around each other.

"You've done nothing wrong. Give me a few days."

Cold fills the pit of my stomach. I've had the "it's me, not you" talk before. I thought Barrett was better, that he'd at least be honest with me, but I've been wrong before.

"If you found someone else, just tell me."

I hate the whine I hear in my voice. Hate the pain that's already ripping through me because no matter how much it tears me apart, I won't stay with a cheating man.

"Christ, Keisha! What the hell are you talking about?"

I swallow.

"Maybe you tired of my body. I know some men find it a novelty to be with plus sized women, but they go back to being with slender women when the novelty wears off."

"What prick spouted that nonsense at you?"

He shoves his chair back, comes round, and grabs my hand.

"What are you going to do? Let me go."

He marches us into the bedroom, shoves everything away from the center of the dresser and stands in front of the mirror there.

"Strip!"

"Barrett, what are you doing?"

"Do it now Keisha, or I'm ripping those clothes off you."

His shirt is on the floor. He removes his pants and underpants as I hesitate over my bra.

Quickly, I pull my shorts down.

"Come here."

Just like that, I'm ready for him. My core clenches and moisture seeps into my panties.

I close the space between us.

"What do you see?"

I clear my throat twice before I can speak. "You're hard."

"I'm so fucking hard, I'm worried I'm going to cream myself before I pleasure you. Who made my cock that way?"

I glance at him. Fire blazes in his eyes, the way it does when he's making love to me.

"Keisha?" He growls.

"Me?"

I'm getting wetter.

"DAMN RIGHT! KEISHA MADE MY COCK AS HARD AS A STEEL ROD."

He grips my shoulders and forces me to turn around, so I'm facing the mirror.

"Wrap your arms around my neck."

"Let's get into bed."

It's one thing for him to see me, but it's another for me to see myself like this.

"No."

I hesitate.

Barrett waits, fiery eyes watching me through the mirror.

I'm too turned on to stop. I wrap my arms around his neck, my fingers brushing against the hair at his nape.

He rips my bra. Then my panties. His eyes don't leave me the whole time. Mine widen as I realize my heart is racing. I can hardly catch my breath.

"See how beautiful your tits are?" He pushes them together, kneading them. "I'll never tire of petting them. Look, Keisha."

I let my gaze wander from the hard planes of his face and the heat in his eyes to my body.

"This is one of my favorite colors." He touches my dark aureoles with his thumbs, still massaging my breasts.

I gasp. They are my breasts, but I don't recognize how arousing they look, thrusting forward against his palms, my nipples as hard as pebbles.

He splays his hand on the swell of my tummy. "I love how soft you are here."

His cock pushes against my back. It's slippery, as if pre-cum is leaking out of it.

"Tilt your hips forward."

I want his fingers down there. But when I obey him, he leans over me and slides his palms up my thighs.

"Your curvy legs are another favorite part of mine."

My eyes follow his every movement. The contrast of my darker body against his lighter one fascinates me.

Finally, his hand touches my clit.

"Tilt a little more."

With two fingers, he spreads my nether lips so the dark little mass that is my engorged clit is clearly visible.

"See? You have the prettiest pussy I've ever seen. You're so wet and pink. Oh, God Keisha, I want to take you now."

He pushes against me. Simultaneously, his fingers stroke me.

I pant and move against him, throwing my head back. I feel so good, I can't keep my eyes open anymore.

Barrett licks my neck, and I convulse. My legs give way, but he holds me. He lays me over the dresser, anchoring my arms there.

In one smooth movement, he enters me.

"Sweet Keisha," he growls.

"I wish you could see how gorgeous your curvy ass is, with me working it as I slide in and out of you."

"I feel it. Barrett, it's so good."

He freezes.

"Don't stop."

"Who's the most beautiful girl in my world?"

"Keisha." I push my butt against him. "Don't stop."

"Say it like you mean it. Who's my girl?" He roars.

"Keisha!"

"I love every part of you, Keisha." He punctuates each word with a thrust so hard my body slides forward on the dresser.

I'm crying now.

"I love you Keisha."

I turn my head so I can see him. "I love you too, Barrett."

He bucks into me, shooting semen up my pussy, and I come again in the most powerful orgasm of my life.

I don't know how long we stay here, panting. After a little while, Barrett lifts me to the bed, holding me in our familiar position.

"I'm destroying our contract. If you try to leave me, I'm going to lock you up and find ways to change your mind," Barrett says.

I lift my head, pet his face and beard.

He tells me about his mom leaving.

My heart breaks for the little boy he was. I rub my face on his chest.

"I no longer want or need that contract. I love my life here with you, Barrett. I love you. I even love Angelina, Seraphina and Isabella. And to me, marriage means forever."

"Good. Because you were made for my hands, my mouth and my cock, Keisha. And I was made for every sexy part of you."

Epilogue

Barrett

Eight Years Later

I'M AT THE STREAM we can see from our house, trying to stay upright as my three kids use all their combined forces to topple me. I roar as I pretend to be a human-stealing beast.

"Give back our sister, you mean troll," Blake shouts. He's only seven, but his body is strong like mine was when I was his age. He yanks my right leg.

His brother, four-year-old Malik, tries to pull my other leg but keeps on falling.

I lift each leg in turns, making it look as if they are gaining ground. It's hard not to laugh because Little Destiny, who's sitting on my shoulders, is giggling when she should be terrified.

"Malik, pull harder, he's nearly down," Blake shouts.

I bend my knees and drop to the soft grass, careful not to let Destiny fall.

"Daddy, higher," she says.

"I have a cookie in my pocket, Destiny." Blake reaches for his sister, who's now desperate to fall into his arms.

I struggle a little more, then put my baby girl on my chest, fall back and allow her brothers to steal her from me.

"I'll live happily with you, Mr. Monster," Keisha drops beside me.

I put my arm around her, and we watch the kids play.

"Let's have more picnic days like this. We can afford to hire help."

"They are growing too fast. I can't believe Destiny is two. It seems like only yesterday; you were giving birth to her."

"Don't remind me."

"I've been keeping my eye out for someone I can trust and will do a good job, and I believe I found someone. I can't wait to take you on our honeymoon."

"Without the kids?"

"You don't think they'll be okay with Verlin, your mom or dad?"

Keisha and Verlin's wife Lucy have become such good friends. We babysit for her and Verlin and alternate hosting sleep overs for the kids.

"It's not that. I just think it might be weird to be apart from them for more than a day."

"I know what you mean," I say.

I love my life with Keisha and my boys and girl so much. I feel like the luckiest man on earth. It's a miracle that Keisha, who loves this mountain like I do, came into my life.

"I still want to go," Keisha says.

"Any particular place?"

We've talked about going on our honeymoon before, but never really nailed down a place.

"Let's talk about it on the porch tonight, when the kids are sleeping. I think they're getting hungry now."

I sit up. Sure enough, they are heading for the picnic Keisha laid out.

"Let's feed our family," I say.

I pull her up and hold her hand as we walk toward our babies.

Fancy more short and steamy instalove Boxsets from Iris West? Check out The O'Connors Of Blossom Ford Books 1-5, the next boxset in the Blossom Ford Collections series.

FREE BOOK

Would you like a free book? Sign up to my mailing list at https://dl.bookfunnel.com/t191w45ryj to receive a copy of Loving My Fake Husband, a Curvy Brides of Blossom Ford Series short story.

HELP OTHERS FIND THIS BOOK

Thank you for reading Curvy Brides Of Blossom Ford Books 5-8. If you enjoyed this book, please help others discover it by leaving a review. Many thanks,

Iris xx

ABOUT THE AUTHOR

Iris West writes short and steamy romance about alpha heroes and the women they can't help falling in love with. She loves reading all types of romance books that have a happy ending and is an avid Kdrama fan.

Follow or like her on Facebook, Instagram, TikTok, BookBub and/or Goodreads.

Printed in Dunstable, United Kingdom